"I'll pick you up at seven. Wear something sexy," Zane told her.

"You're not picking me up," Nicki called after him. "I'll drive myself."

He paused and stared at her. "I never let my date drive herself."

"D-date?"

"Uh-huh."

He flashed her the kind of smile designed to reduce her to a quivering mass. Damn the man—it worked.

"I'm going to show you all my best moves," he said. "You'll be impressed."

Nicki watched him walk out of the room and had a really bad feeling that Zane was right. She was going to be impressed, and where exactly would that leave her?

Zane thought he could knock her socks off. Well, two could play at that game. Maybe if she surprised him, she could get the upper hand for once. Of course, what she would do with it once she had it was another question entirely!

Dear Reader,

As you ski into the holiday season, be sure to pick up the latest batch of Silhouette Special Edition romances. Featured this month is Annette Broadrick's latest miniseries, SECRET SISTERS, about family found after years of separation. The first book in this series is *Man in the Mist* (#1576), which Annette describes as "...definitely a challenge to write." About her main characters, Annette says, "Greg, the wounded lion hero—you know the type— gave me and the heroine a very hard time. But we refused to be intimidated and, well, you'll see what happened!"

You'll adore this month's READERS' RING pick, *A Little Bit Pregnant* (SE#1573), which is an emotional best-friends-turned-lovers tale by reader favorite Susan Mallery. *Her Montana Millionaire* (SE#1574) by Crystal Green is part of the popular series MONTANA MAVERICKS: THE KINGSLEYS. Here, a beautiful socialite dazzles the socks off a dashing single dad, but gets her own lesson in love. Nikki Benjamin brings us the exciting conclusion of the baby-focused miniseries MANHATTAN MULTIPLES, with *Prince of the City* (SE#1575). Two willful individuals, who were lovers in the past, have become bitter enemies. Will they find their way back to each other?

Peggy Webb tantalizes our romantic taste buds with *The Christmas Feast* (SE#1577), in which a young woman returns home for Christmas, but doesn't bargain on meeting a man who steals her heart. And don't miss *A Mother's Reflection* (SE#1578), Elissa Ambrose's powerful tale of finding long-lost family...and true love.

These six stories will enrich your hearts and add some spice to your holiday season. Next month, stay tuned for more page-turning and provocative romances from Silhouette Special Edition.

Happy reading!

Gail Chasan
Senior Editor

Susan Mallery

A LITTLE BIT PREGNANT

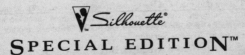

SPECIAL EDITION™

Published by Silhouette Books

America's Publisher of Contemporary Romance

To my real-life Nicki

SILHOUETTE BOOKS

ISBN 0-373-24573-4

A LITTLE BIT PREGNANT

Visit Silhouette at www.eHarlequin.com

Printed in U.S.A.

Books by Susan Mallery

SUSAN MALLERY

is the bestselling and award-winning author of over fifty books for Harlequin and Silhouette Books. She makes her home in the Pacific Northwest with her handsome prince of a husband and her two adorable-but-not-bright cats.

Dear Reader,

Like most Silhouette authors, I'm not just a writer of romances, I'm also a fan. As a reader, I've enjoyed the Silhouette Special Edition READERS' RING books very much and I'm delighted to have a book of mine as part of the collection.

A Little Bit Pregnant is one of those special books that appeared fully formed in my writer's brain. One minute I was searching for a story for Zane, a character from *Shelter in a Soldier's Arms* (SSE #1400), and the next I knew exactly what was going to happen.

Nicki and Zane have a unique relationship. Not just as best friends, but also as soul mates. However, the journey from friends to lovers can be hazardous at best. There is much on the line—if the romantic relationship goes badly, one can lose much more than just a significant other. But if the relationship goes well…is there any greater joy than marrying one's best friend?

I hope you'll enjoy Nicki and Zane's story. Here's to happy endings for us all.

Susan Mallery

Chapter One

"Nicki, I'm desperate. You *have* to help me."

Nicole Beauman heard the impassioned plea over her headset. The words gave her a measure of satisfaction, but weren't impressive enough to make her do much more than blink.

"I'm filing my nails, Zane," she said. "Filing my nails and yawning. That's how impressed I am."

Swearing filled her ears. Despite the seven-hundred-plus miles between her and Zane Rankin, the sound was crystal clear. Modern technology was really amazing.

"My butt is hanging in the wind," Zane told her. "Dammit, Nicki, do something."

He wasn't exactly begging, but it was close enough. Sighing softly, she set down her nail file and glanced at the half dozen monitors on the console.

She'd tapped into the impressive security system of the Silicon Valley computer firm Zane was currently trying to break into. Nearly sixty camera positions showed everything from the six entrances to the lobby to the ''sensitive'' areas. All Nicki has to do was push a couple of buttons to get the view of her choice.

She watched Zane type frantically on a small, portable keyboard that should have unlocked the side door. He knew the sequence of codes to enter, but sometimes these things were tricky, and required a woman's touch.

''Hit clear,'' she told him.

He nodded, pushing a single key, then waited.

She used her keyboard to reenter the codes. When nothing happened, she used a backdoor entry into the security system and unlocked it from the inside. Zane glanced toward the camera monitoring his position and gave her a thumbs-up.

''You're the best,'' he murmured.

''You say that now,'' she told him. ''But yesterday you carefully explained to me how you didn't need my help on this job. You said you were perfectly capable of doing it all on your own.''

''I am.''

''Uh-huh.''

She switched camera positions and saw the security guards heading down the main corridor.

''Then you don't need me to tell you that you're about to have a close encounter with your hosts, right?''

Through the grainy security camera she saw Zane freeze. He glanced up and down the long hallway, then ducked into a room. Five seconds later, the security guards turned the corner and walked past the closed door.

"You're clear," she said when they were out of sight. "And if you have this covered, I'm going to head home."

There was a heavy sigh that originated in the northern California storeroom and made its way to her headset in Seattle.

"What do you want from me?" he asked in resignation.

Nicki grinned at her victory. "Money, but as you're not here to deliver, I'll take an apology."

Zane stepped into the hallway and faced the security camera. "You're the best," he said in a tone of long suffering. "I couldn't do this without you."

She smiled. "You left out the *W* word."

"Wrong. I was wrong. Okay? Now will you get me into the research lab?"

"Of course." She could afford to be gracious in her victory. "It's on the second floor. Take the back stairs and wait on the landing until I give you the all clear."

Five minutes later he was at the door to the research lab. Nicki coaxed the heavy double doors into releasing, then talked Zane through the laser sensors. The safe, hidden in the supply closet, wasn't connected to the main computer system, so she couldn't help with that, but she did temporarily disable the smoke detectors in the lab so the charred smell from the explosion wouldn't set them off.

Zane ducked out of the supply closet and shut the

door. Two seconds later there was a *thud-bang* and the door shuddered. He hurried back inside, only to reemerge with a small black box in his hand.

"Got it," he said, slipping the unit into his backpack. "Now get me out of here."

"I should let you get caught, just to teach you a lesson."

He glanced at the camera and grinned. "But you won't."

He was right, she thought as she located the guards. "Okay. Take the north stairs to the main floor. I'll unlock the front door before you get there. Just breeze on through."

When he was safely speeding away from the building, she reset the security system, cleared the fire alarms and turned them back on, then disconnected from their computer. There was no way to disguise the fact that someone had broken in, but they wouldn't trace the entry back to her. She'd made sure to cover her tracks.

Of course at about nine-fifteen the following morning Zane's partner, Jeff Ritter, was going to review the computer logs for the previous twenty-four hours and find lots of unauthorized searches, entries and activity. To say he would be unamused was putting it mildly. Nicki wondered if there would be an actual explosion of tempers or just fireworks.

"I owe you big time."

Zane's voice came over her headset.

"I know," she told him as she shut down her computer.

He chuckled. "Want me to bring in doughnuts in the morning?"

"That hardly makes up for it, but all right. Don't eat all the glazed this time."

"Promise."

"Ha."

She knew exactly what his doughnut promises meant. She would be lucky to have a glazed crumb to nibble on.

"I'm heading home," she told him.

"Drive safely. And Nicki?"

"Yes?"

"You're the best."

"I know. Night, Zane."

She smiled as she disconnected their call and dropped her headset onto her console.

"I saved you one," Zane said the following morning as he strolled into Nicki's office and placed a glazed doughnut on her desk.

She glanced from it to him and wondered why she'd bothered with coffee. There was no need for caffeine to get her body jump-started—not when she could watch Zane's easy stride and casual smile. The combination always sent her pulse to racing, her blood to boiling and her heart to fluttering. Embarrassing but true.

Being around Zane was nearly as much of a workout as an aerobics class. One of these days she would actually calculate the calorie burn rate. Now if only keeping her crush a secret was a form of strength training, she would be fit enough to kayak around the world.

"What time did you get back last night?" she asked.

"The flight was about ninety minutes. I was sliding into bed shortly before one." He settled on the chair next to her desk and grinned. "Slept like a baby."

"What? No new chickie keeping the sheets warm?"

"Not this week. I need to catch up on my beauty sleep."

Nicki had seen Zane on zero sleep and happened to know he was still way too pretty for her comfort zone. Tall, lean, handsome, with dark hair and deep-set eyes that held too many secrets, he could have made his fortune on the soaps as the hunk of the month.

He was one of those men women found irresistible. While she prided herself on being unique, in this case she was just one of the crowd. The only difference between her and every other woman mooning over Zane's broad shoulders and high, tight fanny was she kept her foolish dreams to herself. He didn't date women with an IQ larger than their bust measurement and she'd been blessed with plenty of smarts. Unfortunately all the brains in the world didn't seem to be an antidote for his particular brand of charm.

"What about you?" he asked, snagging her cup of coffee and taking a sip. "Did Brad wait up for you?"

She grabbed her mug back. "His name is Boyd and no, I didn't see him last night." She hadn't been seeing much of Boyd at all, lately, but she wasn't going to share that with Zane.

Zane raised his eyebrows. "Why not? All that computer jargon getting boring? Seriously, Nicki, don't you get tired of the guy talking in binary code?"

"Boyd isn't a programmer. He's an electrical engineer who—" She broke off in midsentence and shook her head. "Why do I bother? You make fun of the men in my life because you're embarrassed about the women you date. I mean what about Julie?"

Zane chuckled. "Embarrassed? Julie is a former Miss Apple Festival who is studying very hard to be a dental hygienist."

"Right. She's in year four of a nine-month program."

"Math isn't her thing."

"She's going to clean teeth. How much math could there be? What? She can't count high enough to know how many teeth there actually are in someone's mouth?"

"She's gorgeous."

"She's an idiot. Don't you ever want to have a conversation with these women? I mean when the sex is over for the evening, then what?"

He winked. "I go home and sleep. Besides, when I want to have a conversation with a woman, I come see you."

"How flattering." The good old female best friend, Nicki thought with a combination of chagrin and humor. That was her.

"I'm telling you, Nicki, let go of the smart guy

thing," he said. "Find some stud and let him have his way with you."

"No, thanks."

"Why not? You're pretty enough."

"How flattering. Pretty enough? Pretty enough to get a brainless fool who thinks with his biceps? Why would I want to?"

"For the fun."

"I'm into substance, but thanks for the offer."

She would never understand Zane's casual attitude toward the opposite sex. Didn't he want to settle down? But she already knew the answer to that question. In the two years she'd worked for him, she'd never seen Zane get involved with anyone for more than a few weeks. There was always a new airhead on his arm and he didn't seem to care that they were interchangeable.

For her part, she gravitated toward serious men who used their brains. Unfortunately none of them had been appealing enough to get her over her Zane crush. Biceps-Man would be a change, if nothing else.

Oh, like that was going to happen.

"I need to like the guy before I have sex," she said. "Call me old-fashioned, but it's true."

"Fascinating information," Jeff Ritter said as he walked into her office. "Thanks for sharing, but we have more pressing matters."

Nicki winced silently. If she could have picked some part of the conversation for her other boss to overhear, it wouldn't have been that.

Jeff stalked into the glass-enclosed office and slammed the door shut behind him. Nicki braced herself for the explosion while Zane seemed singularly unimpressed. He remained slumped in the chair next to her desk.

"What's up?" he asked.

Jeff tossed him a folder. "What the hell were you thinking? Dammit, Zane, you could have told me what you were going to do."

Zane flipped through the pages of the computer activity report. "You would have told me not to. Technically we're partners and you can't order me around, but you would have tried to convince me it was a bad idea."

Jeff glared at him. "It *was* a bad idea. Do you have any idea how many laws you broke last night."

Nicki figured she might as well join the fray. "I have the actual count, if you'd like it."

Jeff turned his laserlike stare on her. "You're in enough trouble already."

She sighed. "I know. But just for the breaking and entering, and turning off the security system. And the fire alarms." She considered the number. "Okay, so it was a lot of laws."

Zane shot her a grin. She held in a smile. Jeff wasn't amused.

"I'm glad you two think this is so damn funny, but I don't. Our company has a reputation to uphold. We don't go around breaking the law for our own purposes."

Zane raised his eyebrows. Jeff shoved his hands in his pockets. "Only under extreme circumstances," he amended.

"I was helping out a friend," Zane said.

Jeff's gazed narrowed. "You should have told me what you were going to do."

"I couldn't. If it went bad, I didn't want you or anyone in the company implicated."

"Nicki knew," Jeff said.

"Sure, but she'd never say anything."

Zane's casual acceptance of her loyalty was both gratifying and annoying. She felt like the faithful family retainer…or a favorite dog.

"You could have gotten her in a lot of trouble," Jeff said.

For the first time since swaggering into her office, Zane actually squirmed.

"I couldn't have done it without her," he said.

"That's right," she told Jeff. "Zane's pretty useless."

Now they were both glaring at her. She shrugged.

Jeff started to speak, but Zane cut him off. "My friend had been working two years on the prototype. These guys stole it and he wanted it back. I said I'd help him. I had to, Jeff. I owed him."

Nicki knew a few details about Zane's background. He'd been in the Marines where he'd done a lot of things he didn't talk about. Jeff had the same sort of background. Several years ago the two of them met up and started the company.

Neither of them talked about their past, nor did they ever sit around telling war stories. But every now and then, something came out. A new piece of information, a whisper of a truth.

It was there now—in the tone of Zane's voice as he said those three words.

I owed him.

She didn't know what they meant, but Jeff did. Instead of complaining or continuing the questioning, he simply nodded.

"Next time, run it past me, okay?"

Zane rose and nodded. "Promise."

He walked out of the office.

Nicki watched him go. How had Zane owed the guy? Had he saved his life or something? She knew there was no point in asking. Zane was a master at avoiding topics he didn't want to talk about.

Jeff turned his attention back to her. "You could at least *pretend* to be worried that I'm going to fire you."

"You can't. Not over this. I work for Zane and he needed my help. My job is to provide backup, not to pass judgment on what he's doing."

Jeff sighed. "You're too smart for your own good."

"You like that I'm smart."

"Yeah, well, you're okay. When you're not being a pain."

She grinned. "Is Zane in trouble? Are you going to punish him? Can I watch?"

One corner of Jeff's mouth twitched. "You two deserve each other. I have a meeting with a client. Someone who's going to pay us for protecting him and his family."

"Good luck."

"Thanks."

She turned back to her computer. Zane walked by

and stuck his head in her office. "How about lunch? Mexican. You can buy."

"I want Chinese and this one is on you, bucko."

He shook his head. "All right. But only because you're crabby. Brad must not be putting out this week."

"His name is Boyd," she yelled after him.

"Whatever," he called as he headed down the hall.

She considered chasing after him, but then what? It wasn't polite to run down her boss.

Nicki turned in her wheelchair and rolled over to the file cabinet under the window. As she flipped through the folders, she told herself that she simply had to get over her crush and pronto. Boyd was a perfectly nice guy, and if not for her weakness for Zane, she might have fallen in love with him. That was what she wanted—to have one great man in her life, to settle down, get married, do the kid thing.

But until she found a way to get over Zane, she was stuck in limbo—wanting what she couldn't have and having what she didn't want.

"The Seahawks by three," Zane said over a plate of Kung Pao Beef and rice.

Nicki grinned. "You lead with your chin. You should know better. I'll take those three points, and listen to you whine come Monday morning."

She noted the information on a sheet of paper that listed all the pro football games for the weekend.

Zane knew taking the Seahawks wasn't smart, but he couldn't help rooting for the home team. Nicki had no such loyalty. She studied stats, read the sports section and made her choices based on abilities, injuries and who was on a winning streak. Every now and then she took a team because she liked their uniforms, but not often. What killed him was even when she made her choices on something as stupid as team colors, she often won. They were only two weeks into the regulation season and she was already up by three games.

They didn't bet money. Instead they keep a running total and whoever had the most wins at the end of the season owed the loser a day of slave labor. The previous season he'd had big plans to make her cook, stocking his freezer with homemade dinners. Instead he'd spent nearly eight hours washing and waxing her van. Afterwards, he'd been sore for three days.

"I'm going to have you paint my living room," she said dreamily as she wrote down the rest of their picks. "I'm thinking of a color-wash treatment that's going to take at least three coats of paint."

He shook his head. "Not this time, sweet pea. You're going to be cooking your heart out."

"That's what you said last year. Do we remember what happened instead?"

"I'd rather not."

She grinned. "You've got to start listening to the experts, Zane. They usually know who's going to win the games."

"That's cheating."

"No, that's beating your fanny."

She grinned as she spoke. Laughter danced in her green eyes. He smiled back.

"You're smart for a girl."

She picked up her fork and leaned forward. "You left out pretty. Earlier you said I was pretty enough to get some macho, brainless guy with huge muscles."

He studied her heart-shaped face. With big eyes and a full, sensual mouth, she was more than pretty. Long auburn curls cascaded down her back. Every swaying movement begged a man to run his fingers through them. Put all that on a body that, while not as lush as the women he dated, had all the right curves in exactly the right places and she was a serious contender.

"You're okay," he said.

She laughed. "Wait. I want to pause and savor this moment for as long as possible. The wildly extravagant compliment has gone to my head."

He pointed his fork at her. "Come on, Nicki. You know you're attractive. Half the guys in this place can't take their eyes off you."

"Only half?" She glanced around. "I suppose that's something."

He followed her gaze and saw a couple of businessmen in tailored suits giving her the once-over. There were three college guys in the corner. They practically had their mouths hanging open.

"I rest my case," he said.

"Their attention will last for a long as it takes us to finish our meal and head for the door."

He frowned. "Because of the chair?"

She shrugged. "Well, duh. What do you think?"

"That you're crazy. They're not going to care."

Nicki being in a wheelchair meant that she was

faster than him and more likely to run him over if she was annoyed. But it didn't make her any less attractive.

"It doesn't bother Brad," he said.

"Boyd. And you're right. It doesn't. But he's into substance."

"I'm not and it doesn't bother me."

She rolled her eyes. "That's because we're friends. You wouldn't date a woman in a wheelchair."

He considered the statement. "I would if she had really big breasts."

Nicki shook her head. "I don't know if I should thank you or stab you with my knife."

"Technically you work for me. If you tried to stab me it would reflect poorly on your next evaluation."

"You drive me crazy."

He grinned. "I know. Isn't it great?"

When they'd finished lunch and she'd badgered him into paying, he stood and she pushed back from the table. Zane paused to watch the men in the restaurant.

None of them had noticed the sleek wheelchair. Nicki had hers specially made by a guy in California. It was lightweight, made to fit her slender body and more low-profile than most.

The college guys exchanged a look of surprise, shrugged and continued to stare. One of the businessmen turned away, but the other looked as if his eyes were about to fall out. Just as he'd thought. Most of them didn't care.

He followed her into the parking lot. She hit the remote on her key chain, which activated the special motor installed in back. The rear doors of the van opened and a ramp lowered. Nicki rolled onto it and rose to level with the back of the vehicle. While he slid into the passenger side, she secured the back doors and moved in behind the steering wheel. Special grooves locked her chair into place and a custom-built harness acted as a seat belt. She started the engine.

"They were still looking," he said conversationally.

"I'm not," she told him.

"Brad isn't all that."

She sighed. "Boyd, Zane. His name is Boyd. You'll be meeting him in a couple of nights at the Morgans' party. Please try to remember his name by then."

"I'll do my best."

"Who are you bringing? Miss Apple Festival?"

He shrugged. Currently he was between women. Oddly enough, he was in no hurry to find a new one, either. He glanced at Nicki. The two of them had never been uninvolved at the same time. Not that he would ask her out if they were. Nicki was...

He glanced out the window. Nicki was special. She mattered to him and he made it a rule to never get involved with anyone fitting that description. Not again.

Chapter Two

"So the guy says, 'It's only a parrot.'" Rob, one of the burly bodyguards employed by the company laughed as he finished telling his joke.

Nicki rolled her eyes and smiled. Rob loved telling jokes nearly as much as he loved puns. At times conversations with him were physically painful as he went from pun to pun.

"You're not sweating, Nicki," Ted called. "I want to see you sweat."

"Bite me," Nicki yelled back as she picked up the pace on the recumbent bike. Her thigh muscles ached, but in a good way. As for sweat, there was a river of it pouring down her back.

She hated aerobics. Oh sure, they were good for her heart and probably added years to her life, but she loathed them with a cheerful intensity that never faded. Unlike Zane, who thought all forms of physical activity were pure play.

Speaking of which, he chose that moment to stroll into the company gym. The bodyguards called out a greeting. Nicki ignored him because looking at him would spike her blood pressure and set off alarms.

But as he approached, she couldn't resist a quick peek at his long bare legs, the loose gym shorts and cutoff T-shirt that exposed way too much flat, sculpted tummy. The man had a serious body.

She would have accepted that with good grace if she'd been able to study it impersonally. As if he were nothing more than fine art. *Very* fine art. But what she resented most was her visceral reaction to that A+ set of abs. She *wanted*. Yup, physical cravings set in that made the PMS need for chocolate seem wimpy by comparison.

"Hey," he said as he slumped down into her wheelchair. "You're not sweating."

"That's what I said," Ted told him as he straightened and grabbed a towel. "The girl's loafing."

"The *woman* is busting her butt," Nicki complained.

Zane ignored her. "I called you last night and you were out. How's Brad?"

His hips were narrow enough to allow him to easily fit on her custom seat, but his legs were miles too long. He stretched them out in front of him and rested his heels on the hardwood floor.

"*Boyd* is doing great," she said. "Thanks for asking. But I didn't see him last night."

"So where were you?"

"So why do you get to know?"

He grinned. "Because I'm fifteen kinds of charming and you adore me."

He had that one nailed.

"I was at the bookstore."

"Why not with your computer geek?"

"He's in the middle of a big project right now."

Zane looked anything but convinced. "Sure he is. You're bored. Admit. You think he's tedious."

"I think you're overcompensating because of personal inadequacy."

Rob and Ted finished their workouts and left. Zane glanced at the timer on her bike's program. "Your mom sent me cookies."

"She mentioned she was going to."

Nicki found a certain amount of irony in the fact that her parents were nearly as taken with Zane as she was. Maybe it was something genetic. A weakness in the Beauman family tree.

"So when are they coming up for a visit?" he asked.

"Probably not until the holidays. They're taking off for a cruise in Australia and New Zealand at the end of the month. It's fall here, but spring down under."

"You need to have me over for dinner while they're here. I like your folks."

"Me, too."

He grinned.

What the man could do to her with just a smile.

"Is their remodeling finished?" he asked.

"Just about. Mom promised the guest room would be done in time for my next visit."

Nicki had been a change-of-life baby and a surprise for a couple who had given up hope of ever having a child. As such, she'd been doted on from birth. Despite their devotion, they'd been ready to retire as she finished college. They'd left Seattle for the sunny warmth of Tucson, which gave her a good excuse to flee the incessant rain every winter.

"Maybe I'll swing down and visit them sometime," he said.

"They'd like that."

Her mother especially. While Muriel Beauman would have adored Zane for his own sake, she had a special place in her heart for him because of how he treated her daughter. When her parents had met Zane, her mother had made it a point to tell Nicki that he didn't seem to notice she was in a wheelchair.

Nicki knew that was true. Zane's acceptance was complete. Sometimes she consoled herself that his lack of interest in her had nothing to do with her problems with her legs. Nope, it was her pesky brain getting in the way.

The timer on her bike beeped. Nicki slowed, then stopped and wiped the sweat from her face. Her muscles were comfortably tired, but her workout was just beginning.

Still in the wheelchair, Zane moved next to the bike. "Climb on," he said as he wrapped one arm around her waist.

She relaxed as he pulled her onto his lap and "drove" her to the weight machines clustered at the far end of the room. This was a familiar part of their routine—one she tried not to get excited about. Yeah, he had his arm around her. Yeah, it felt good. So what?

She slid from Zane's lap to the bench. He locked the wheelchair in place and rose.

While she hooked up the elaborate pulley system that allowed her to strengthen her leg muscles without putting too much weight on them, he moved to the treadmill where he punched in his favorite program. The machine started at a warm-up pace that would send most people into cardiac arrest. Zane wouldn't even begin breathing hard until mile three.

She might hate exercise, Nicki thought as she began the leg lifts designed by a physical therapist to keep her lower body toned and flexible, but there were compensations. One was a boss who'd had no problem adding a couple of pieces of equipment to the company gym so she could work out there as well. The other was watching Zane move.

Mirrors covered all four walls so wherever she turned, she saw front and back views of the man. The machine picked up the pace and he eased from a jog into a full-out run. Long, lean muscles bunched and released with nearly balletlike grace. Nicki mentally smacked herself upside the head and returned her attention to her own workout.

"Jeff and I are having a planning meeting later today," Zane called to her. "Any preferences?"

Employees were often allowed to request assignments so those with families could stay close to home and those without could indulge their wanderlust.

"I'd like to winter in Hawaii," Nicki told him.

He grinned. "I don't think we have any clients there."

"Then we should get some. Maybe a pro football player or a surfing champion."

"Maybe a suntan lotion model."

Nicki sniffed. "Not at all my style."

She released the pulleys and turned so her legs

hung off the bench. When she was in position, she began to work her upper body.

Strong muscles were essential for a number of reasons. Not only did they help her maneuver and stay fast in her chair, but well-toned arms burned more calories. She might be able to keep in shape with her workouts, but she didn't have the ability to walk from place to place during the day. If she wasn't careful to balance her exercise with her lifestyle, she could pile on five pounds in the time it took most people to sneeze. On her smallish frame, that was hardly attractive. So she did the exercise thing and told herself it was like taking a really sweaty vitamin.

Zane finished his five-mile run and stepped off the treadmill. As she shifted from the bench to her wheelchair, he nodded to the free weights and barbells.

"Want me to spot you on the chest press?" he asked.

Nicki eyed the equipment in question. Did she want to lay on a bench, Zane poised at her head, ready to rescue her if she got into trouble as she raised and lowered a too-heavy weight? The view was spectacular—she could see all of him from knee to chin—but it came at a price. Namely unfulfilled fantasies.

"I'll pass," she said as she headed for the women's locker room and the showers. "But thanks."

"No problem."

He turned to the equipment and began his own weight training. Nicki didn't want to stick around. She'd seen the show countless times. If only she could be like Zane, she thought as she rolled to her locker. If only she could be happy with them just being friends and never consider any other possibilities. If only he didn't bother her so much.

She needed a plan. Or a program. Or an anti-Zane patch. Barring that, she had to find a way to clear her head. Boyd might not be the love of her life, but what if the next guy was? Would she miss her opportunity because she was hung up on Zane? Wouldn't that be a tragedy?

She was going to have to find a way to lick this problem once and for all, even if it meant something as drastic as finding a new job.

"This client is interesting," Jeff said as he tossed Zane a folder.

Zane picked it up and flipped through the pages. "An Italian banker?" He grinned. "Okay. I'll take that one."

Jeff didn't look surprised. "You think you're going to get a trip to Italy out of this."

"Sure."

Jeff shook his head and passed over two more folders. "Middle Eastern oil executives."

"A whole lot less fun," Zane muttered as he looked through their files. "Definitely more work."

Although he wouldn't mind a good distraction— maybe a kidnapping or hostage situation. He felt restless and on edge and he couldn't say why.

"Westron has had a couple of nasty letters delivered to his house," Jeff said. "He annoyed the wrong group of people."

"Death threats?" Zane asked.

"Daily. He's working with local police, but he wants us to come up with a plan to protect the family he has here in the States."

Zane made a few notes in the margin. When the company first started, he and Jeff had shared the work equally. In the past couple of years Jeff had taken over more administrative and sales duties, leaving much of the field work to Zane. The switch had come about because of Jeff's marriage to a single mom and the subsequent birth of his son. Little Michael was nearly eighteen months old.

"How's Ashley?" he asked.

Jeff's expression softened as he smiled. "Great. She's still getting morning sickness, but if this pregnancy is like the last one, it should pass in a few more weeks."

He continued talking, but Zane found himself unable to listen. Instead he fought against ghosts from the past, and the pain they brought with him.

He was happy for his friend, he told himself. As for his own life, it had turned out the way it had and there was not a damn thing he could do about it. Once he'd thought he could have a normal life, then he'd found out he was wrong. End of story.

He returned his attention to his partner's conversation and made notes on the various files. When they were finished, he headed for Nicki's office and found her on the phone.

He leaned against the door frame and waited as she chewed out whoever had annoyed her. Watching Nicki mad was a kick.

"You can't be serious," she said, using both hands to gesture, even though the person on the other end of her headset couldn't see. "If I'd wanted a cheap piece of crap, that's what I would have ordered. Instead I ordered an expensive transmitter that was supposed to have a two-mile radius. The one I received has a radius of about three hundred yards. Now I'm not a math person, but even I can figure out that's not close to one mile let alone two. So what are you going to do about this?''

She listened, sighed impatiently, then rolled her eyes. Her frustration made him grin. Nicki had a lot of great qualities but suffering fools gladly wasn't one of them.

He watched the fire flashing in her eyes and the way her mouth moved as she spoke. As always, he acknowledged her beauty with the same emotional attachment he had to the weather. It was a part of his world. He lived with it, prepared for it when he re-membered and had absolutely no control over it. So mostly he ignored it.

''You'd better credit me the shipping cost,'' she muttered. ''Yeah, I know. This is your last chance. One more screwup like this and I'm taking my size-able budget elsewhere. Uh-huh.'' She listened for an-other couple of seconds, then said goodbye and hung up.

She glanced at Zane. ''He actually had the nerve to tell me to have a nice day. My day was doing great right up until I found out about the messed-up order. People can be so annoying.''

''Maybe it's not people. Maybe it's you.''

Her gaze narrowed. ''Easy for you to say. You del-egate all the annoying stuff to me.''

''One of the perks of the job.'' He waved a folder. ''I have some exciting news.''

She didn't look convinced. ''Sure you do.''

''Nicki. I'm not kidding. But I'm not going to tell you until I see the proper level of enthusiasm.''

She drew in a breath and clutched both hands to her chest. ''Oh, Zane. Exciting news? I just can't wait.'' Her voice was a falsely high pitch that could have called dogs from three states away. "Wait. I'm all flustered. Let me sit down and recover for a second."

She fluttered her fingers and quivered in her chair.

He chuckled, then sank into the seat by her desk. "It's not the world that's annoying," he told her. "It's you."

"Sell it somewhere else. What have you got?"

He handed her the top folder. "New client. An Italian banker. I'm going to be talking to him about setting up a better security plan for his family."

Nicki's green eyes widened. "Will you be visiting him yourself?"

"I just may. And if I do, I'll need an assistant."

She flipped through the pages and smiled. "I love Italy. It's so beautiful and do they know how to make wine or what? I haven't been in years."

"Did you go with your folks?"

"When I was in high school. Then I went with a bunch of friends while I was in college."

"With a guy?"

She raised her eyebrows. "There might have been a man or two in the group. I simply can't remember."

"Liar."

"Are you inquiring about my sex life?"

"Absolutely."

She pretended to be shocked. "A lady never kisses and tells."

"I'm not interested in the kissing. Do it anywhere interesting?"

"I'm not into public displays of affection, thank you very much." She closed the folder. "My big complaint is that despite promises to the contrary, not one man in Italy pinched my butt."

He shook his head. "Did you ever think it might have something to do with you being in a wheelchair? It's not exactly easy to pinch when the butt in question is planted on a seat. You should have worn your braces a couple of days and given the guys a chance."

"Good point. Honestly, I never thought it would be worth the effort."

"That's because you haven't had your butt pinched by a professional."

"Are you offering?"

"It's not my fantasy, but I could ask around if you'd like."

Nicki pushed the folder toward him. "You are too weird for words. Yes, if asked, I will accompany you to Italy. Now get out of here. Unlike the rest of you, I have actual work that needs to be done."

The Friday morning planning meeting lasted over two hours. As per the usual schedule, the least pressing clients were discussed first, leaving the most time for those with the largest and most imminent problems.

Oil executives stationed in the Middle East should know better than to make political statements, Nicki thought as she listened to Jeff outline the situation. There had been daily threats against George Westron and his family ever since he'd told an AP reporter that most of the area's problems could be solved if people simply practiced Christian values.

But the man being an idiot didn't mean he should be killed by a car bomb or that his family should suffer, either.

Jeff passed Nicki copies of the threats left on the Westron's front porch. She scanned the block letters taken from various magazines and newspapers, then glued into words and sentences.

"Obviously there is an entire international task force working on that," he told her. "But see what you can do."

Nicki nodded. She wasn't an expert, but she had contacts who were. People outside of mainstream law enforcement. Sometimes she got lucky. She also noted a list of information Jeff wanted cross-referenced.

"There are two children," Zane said, when Jeff had finished. "Twelve and ten."

Nicki winced. She hated when kids were in danger. "Tell me they're not still going to school."

He nodded. "It's private. We have two guys with them the entire day."

She shook her head. While she understood the need to keep kids' lives as normal as possible, the knowledge that they were out in the open, *exposed* put a knot in her stomach.

Zane didn't look any happier than she felt. He shrugged. "I sent in Mathews and Gorson."

Some of her tension eased. Those two were great with kids and seemed to have a sixth sense about danger. Zane would have chosen them for that reason. He sweated when kids were in danger, too. Jeff worried, but he *had* kids of his own so she expected it. The same level of concern from Zane always left her weak in the knees…figuratively *and* literally.

She reminded herself she should be looking for reasons not to like Zane, not more excuses to fall harder for the guy. But it was difficult to dislike him. He was too close to perfect for her comfort.

Jeff finished up his report and asked for questions.

When there weren't any, he reminded them that there was a new batch of bodyguards starting training on Monday, so they needed to stay sharp.

Nicki knew that new recruits were often ambushed while walking through the halls of the company. Once a fake terrorism team had invaded and taken hostages. She'd been caught in a standoff for nearly a half hour, which wouldn't have been a problem if she hadn't been on her way to the bathroom in the first place. She made a mental note to be more careful about her water consumption during the next few weeks.

Brenda, Jeff's fifty-something assistant, rose and glared at her boss. "I can't believe you didn't consider my application. *Again.*"

Zane glanced at Nicki and grinned. "Here we go," he murmured.

Brenda's desire to be a real live spy was an ongoing source of humor in the office.

Jeff rose and patted her on the arm. "Brenda, I can't risk losing you. Not only would your husband kill me, but the office would fall apart. You're too valuable for field work."

"That's a crock and you know it," she said, following him from the room. "Come on, Jeff. Just give me a chance."

Nicki watched her go. "I'm always torn," she admitted to Zane as the rest of the staff filed out of the conference room. "On the one hand I know Jeff is right—Brenda does keep things running smoothly. But on the other hand, she should be allowed to live up to her potential."

"She would never pass the physical."

"Fine. Then let her take it and fail. At least she would have had the chance."

Zane didn't look convinced, which made Nicki suspicious. "You and Jeff are afraid she *will* pass and then you'd have to let her into the program. You know she'd kick butt once she was accepted."

"You're a troublemaker."

"I prefer to think of myself as a rebel. Sort of like a freedom fighter for people who are being oppressed by those in power. Those who have never—"

The phone on the table buzzed. "Nicki, you have a call on line three."

"Thank God," Zane muttered. "I couldn't stand another one of those speeches on the oppressed."

"I'm not finished with you," she said as she picked up the receiver."

"This is Nicki," she said, then felt her mood deflate when she heard Boyd's voice. He wasn't the kind of guy who checked in during the day "just because." Which meant there was only one reason he was calling.

"I'm really sorry I can't make it tonight," he told her. "But with Stan quitting, the project is at risk. I don't want it to fall behind."

He went on about some particularly complex problem that made no sense to her after the first three words. When he paused for breath, she spoke up.

"It's okay, Boyd. Tonight is just a party. Don't worry about it."

"I'll call you in a few days," he said. "After the weekend." He seemed to realize that most couples who were dating actually spent time together on weekends and quickly added, "I have to work."

"I guessed that. It's fine."

More than fine, she thought sadly as she hung up. She didn't feel regret or sadness or anything. For the past couple of weeks she'd been telling herself it was time to end things with Boyd. Whatever potential had been there had obviously been lost. This conversation told her it was *past* time to make a clean break.

"That's the thing," Zane said as he leaned toward her. "Guys like Brad just don't appreciate women. Computer chips and binary code are more interesting. Crazy, but true."

She closed her eyes and counted to ten. When that didn't help, she opened her eyes and glared at him. "*Boyd* isn't a programmer and he's plenty interested in woman and—" She laughed. "Why on earth am I trying to convince you?"

"I have no idea. I don't have a date, either. We can go together."

Nicki told herself that the sudden flash of heat that zinged up her thighs was little more than the beginnings of some kind of rash. Or a food allergy. It wasn't excitement about Zane's offhand invitation. So he was between women. That happened all the time. Just as quickly, he would be involved again with a large-breasted, slow-witted beauty whose most challenging conversational gambit would be to discuss the various shades of teal that went with her eyes.

"I suppose I could hang out with you at the party," she said with a casual deliberateness she didn't come close to feeling. At this moment in time, her insides were practicing clog dancing.

"Hey, I'll even pick you up," he said.

She thought about his flashy two-seater sports car and grinned. "I think tying my wheelchair to your bumper and dragging it behind would be a really bad idea."

"Don't sweat the details, Nicki. I'll take care of

everything." He rose and headed for the door. "I'll pick you up at seven. Wear something sexy."

"You're not picking me up," she called after him. "Don't be silly. I'll drive myself."

He paused in the doorway and stared at her. "I never let my date drive herself."

Her throat didn't just get tight. No, first it twisted up like a spring. "D-date?"

"Uh-huh."

He flashed her the kind of smile deigned to reduce her to a quivering mass. Damn the man—it worked.

"I'm going to show you all my best moves," he said. "You'll be impressed."

Nicki watched him walk out of the room and had a really bad feeling that Zane was right. She was going to be impressed and where exactly would that leave her? The last thing she needed was to be *more* attracted to him.

Then she reminded herself she'd never been the sort of person to walk away from a challenge. Zane thought he could knock her socks off. Well, two could play at that game. He'd told her to wear something sexy. She could do that and then some. Maybe if she surprised him, she could get the upper hand for once. Of course what she would do with it once she had it was another question entirely.

Chapter Three

Nicki stared into the full-length mirror and wondered if she was making a mistake. Yes, she wanted to impress Zane, but maybe she was going about it all wrong. She might be attractive and all that, but there was no way on earth her size-B breasts could compete in the major leagues. Zane dated women who were so top heavy they couldn't walk straight.

She glanced from her reflection to her chest and back. In her closet was a black dress with a neckline that sank nearly to her navel. With some double stick tape and a very straight back, she could dazzle. But in a world of watermelons, who bothered with peaches? Maybe this choice was better. Simple, elegant and classy. Wasn't that better than trying too hard?

Nicki wished desperately for a second opinion, but her mom was in another state and Ashley, Jeff's wife, was busy getting herself ready. Besides, there wasn't much her friend could tell her over the phone.

"You look great," Nicki said in an effort to make herself feel better.

She knew she didn't look bad at all. The shimmering bronze fabric of her dress draped beautifully. The loose boat-style neckline left her arms bare— arms that were toned. Folds of fabric hinted at the curves of her breasts without actually exposing them. Her skin was pale and she'd chosen to leave it bare, even her legs. Instead of panty hose, she'd smoothed on a lotion with a hint of glimmer.

One advantage of her wheelchair was she never had to worry about sore feet so she wore strappy impractical shoes that would have crippled anyone trying to walk. A cascade of curls that had taken nearly twenty minutes to arrange and spray into place tumbled down her back.

Had her date been anyone but Zane, she would have been pleased with her appearance. But seeing as it was him... She pressed a hand to her fluttering stomach and tried to think calming thoughts.

"Not a date," she whispered. "This is not a date. It's two friends hanging out together. But if it were a date..."

She allowed herself a minute or two of pure fantasy. Zane walking in the door, being so swept away that he pulled her into his arms and kissed her senseless. Then their clothes dissolved and they were making love on the rug in front of the fire.

Of course there were several problems with her fantasy. First of all, she was in a wheelchair and pulling her into his arms could be complicated. Second, the fireplace wasn't lit, nor was there a rug in front of it. Somehow making love on a hardwood floor wasn't very appealing.

Maybe she shouldn't have attended that job fair after college. If she hadn't met Jeff and been intrigued by his Ritter/Rankin Security, she would have pursued a post-graduate degree in psychology. With professional training she would be able to handle her crush on Zane. Of course if she'd gone to grad school she never would have met him and how gray her world would be without his light.

"Decisions, decisions," she murmured as she wheeled out of her bedroom.

The doorbell rang just in time to offer a distraction. She headed in that direction and pulled it open.

She'd known Zane was going to pick her up—he'd insisted. And she'd been aware that by him coming to her house, she would be forced to look at him. She'd even told herself he would look good. Unfortunately she'd underestimated the situation by about forty-five percent.

He didn't look good, he looked amazing. While he usually wore suits at work, the one he had on tonight was more elegant or better tailored or something. The smooth gray fabric brought out the depth of his eyes and made his shoulders look about two miles wide. He'd showered, shaved and wore the burgundy and silver tie she'd given him for Christmas the previous year.

Her brain registered all that before she noticed the spray of flowers he held in one hand. And not just flowers. Nothing traditional like roses or carnations. Instead Zane held several stalks of delicately beautiful orchids. The pale creamy petals were alabaster, tinged with muted green.

"Hey, Nicki," Zane said as he stepped into her entryway. "You look beautiful, but I expected that." He handed her the flowers. "I chose these because they reminded me of you."

As he bent toward her, he brushed her cheek with his mouth. Tingles shot through her like out-of-control fireworks.

She couldn't think, couldn't move. Fortunately, it didn't matter if she swayed a little. She was already sitting down and if she collapsed in a heap, the floor wasn't that far away.

"Thank you," she murmured, not sure if she meant the flowers, the compliment or his presence. Maybe she meant it for all of them.

"Shall we put these in water before we go?" he asked.

She nodded and led the way to the kitchen.

The room had been customized with lower cabinets and nothing essential above the countertop. As she didn't get many flowers, the vases were stored in an upper cabinet. She pointed to the right one and Zane got a container down for her. After filling it with water, he retrieved the flowers and set them in the vase.

"They're lovely," she said.

He winked. "Do I know my moves or what?"

"You're a pro," she told him, and meant it. He was a man who knew his way around women. Okay, so they were just friends going out to a work party. But maybe she could allow herself to live in the fantasy for a few hours and pretend this was all real. As long as she didn't get her heart engaged, what could it hurt?

She smiled at him. "You're wearing my tie."

"I know." He touched the length of silk. "Maybe

later you could let me tie you up with it." He wiggled his eyebrows as he spoke.

She laughed and tapped her chair. "I'm at enough of a disadvantage already."

"Want to tie me up instead?"

More than he could know. "I'll think about it," she said instead.

He followed her to the front door. When she wheeled out she was surprised to see an SUV parked at the curb.

"You couldn't possibly have traded your car in on that," she said. "Is it a rental?"

"Nope. I borrowed it from Ashley. Pretty slick, huh?"

It was more than slick. It was a regular car, which meant there was no way she could get inside on her own. Before Nicki could worry about the awkwardness of the moment, Zane had opened the passenger door and scooped her into his arms. He lifted her into the seat.

For the moment, they were at eye level. In the overhead interior light she could see the flecks of gold and amber that sparkled in his dark brown irises. There was a tiny scar by the corner of his mouth and shadows hollowing his cheekbones.

All she could think was that she wanted him to kiss her. Which was crazy, so what she said instead was, "You didn't have to borrow her car. I could have driven."

Zane pulled the seat belt around her and clicked it into place. "No way. On a date, guys drive."

"That is wildly sexist."

He winked. "I know."

The door closed and he moved to the rear of the

vehicle where he collapsed her wheelchair and slid it into the back. When he sat next to her, he grinned.

"Is this the most fun you've had in weeks or what?"

She knew she should have answered "Or what." At the very least she should have acted bored, mentioned Boyd or pretended none of this mattered. Instead she found herself a quivering mass of Zane-lust weakened female hormones.

"It's pretty fun," she admitted.

His smile turned promising. "There's more."

Nicki had never been much of a drinker, but she was a sucker for the occasional glass of champagne. And when it was expensive and served in an actual crystal glass, how could she say no? So she sat in her chair and sipped, while enjoying herself at the party.

There were about forty people in attendance, half of them the staff from Ritter/Rankin Security while the other half were employees of their host.

A few months ago Al Morgan had come to Zane and Jeff after his firm was targeted by a foreign group trying to steal proprietary technology. A sting had been hatched, the culprits apprehended and all was well. The party was a big thank-you to the security firm.

"More?" Zane asked, nodding at her half-full glass.

Nicki shook her head. "I don't like to get too buzzed. You know what they say about drinking and driving." She tapped the arm of her wheelchair as she spoke.

Zane smiled. "I could be your designated driver. I

think you'd look cute drunk.'' He leaned close. ''A few sexy moves in that dress and you'd cause a riot.''

His low, velvet voice brushed against her bare skin and made her want to swoon. He'd been at it all night—staying close, teasing in the most delicious way, gazing at her as if she were the only woman in the room. While she liked the attention, even as she knew it was dangerous to see it as significant, she couldn't help wondering *why* he was doing it. Bringing her flowers was one thing, but actually spending the evening in date mode was something else.

''Move over big guy,'' Ashley Ritter said as she walked up to the sofa.

Zane stood. ''I'll grab us some food,'' he said, then leaned toward Ashley and kissed her on the cheek. ''You're radiant as always.''

''If you think that shamelessly flattering your partner's wife is going to influence how I talk about you, you're right,'' she said as she settled on the sofa. ''Bring me back anything salty please.''

He nodded and headed for the buffet. Nicki frowned at her friend. ''Aren't you supposed to be watching sodium? Didn't you swell up like a balloon when you were pregnant with Michael?''

Jeff's wife wrinkled her nose, then brushed back her dark hair. ''Thanks so much for reminding me.''

''I'm your friend. I worry.''

Ashley sighed. ''I know I have to watch my diet but in the past couple of days I've been like a cow without a salt lick. Desperate.'' Her hazel eyes danced with amusement. ''But enough about the oddities of my pregnant self. What's going on with you? Since when did Zane start escorting you to parties and hanging on your every word and why didn't you call and tell me he'd finally seen the light?''

Nicki instinctively turned to make sure Zane was safely across the room and not within hearing distance. ''It's not like that,'' she said, her voice low. ''Boyd couldn't make it tonight and Zane offered to bring me. Nothing more.''

''That's not what it looks like to me, young lady.''

Nicki sighed. ''He's on date patrol or something, but it doesn't mean anything.''

Ashley's expression turned sympathetic. She leaned close. ''I know you're convinced he couldn't possibly be interested in you because he only dates bubbleheads, but I think you should tell him the truth about your feelings and give this whole thing a chance. Zane is a lot like Jeff—there's plenty concealed beneath the surface. The difference is Jeff hid himself behind the walls of being a warrior while Zane chooses a more charming facade. But that doesn't change the reality. They're both hiding the real man.''

''Who is the real Zane?'' Nicki asked. ''Sometimes I think I catch glimpses of him when we're hanging out together. He lets his guard down, which I appreciate. But there's no telling that the inner Zane will be any more interested in me than the outer one.''

''You could try to find out.''

A good plan, Nicki thought, except she wasn't sure she really wanted to know. Not if the answer was negative.

Ashley read her expression. ''So go another route,'' her friend suggested. ''Find out about the secrets he hides. Why does he pursue young women with minimal IQs?''

"Because they're easy."

Ashley chuckled. "Tell him you could be, too. And if you do see him naked, I want a full report."

Nicki grinned. "You always say that but if I ever try to give you details, you can't stand to hear them."

"I know. I get shy."

Nicki thought about the affectionate glances she'd seen between Ashley and Jeff, and the very hot kiss she'd accidentally interrupted one afternoon at the office.

"Not with Jeff," she said.

Ashley sighed. Her expression softened and her gaze sought out her husband. "No, not with Jeff," she agreed.

Zane grabbed a fresh glass of champagne from the server's tray and handed it to Nicki. She took the offered drink.

"Hmm, why do I know this puts me over my limit?" she asked.

He winked.

"You're trying to get me drunk."

"I'll admit the thought crossed my mind," he told her.

"I wouldn't have thought you would have to resort to cheap tricks with your dates."

"I don't," he said smugly. "The women I go out with fall at my feet."

"Easier for me to do that than most, but don't hold your breath."

She grinned as she spoke, then sipped her drink. Zane tucked a loose curl behind her ear.

Laughter brightened her eyes. He'd always found her attractive, but dressed to kill she was stunning.

He'd seen her legs countless times—in the gym, when she wore shorts in the summer. He was used to the long, lean length of thigh and calf. He barely noticed the faint crisscrossing of scars that patterned her right leg. She kept herself in shape and he'd always been man enough to appreciate the curves.

But tonight something was different. Maybe it was the length of her skirt—the way the filmy fabric barely covered the tops of her thighs. Maybe it was the faint glow of her skin, or the fact that when he'd lifted her into the SUV his hand had cupped bare, warm flesh. Whatever the reason, he couldn't stop looking at her legs…or wanting to touch them.

He knew she could feel everything. Her being in a wheelchair wasn't about being paralyzed. So if he stroked his fingers from ankle to knee, then knee to thigh, she would feel every millimeter of contact. And then what? Would she lean toward him, her mouth parting in welcome? Would her breathing quicken as she—

"Zane?"

Nicki's voice called him back to the party.

He blinked and forced his mind away from her body. "What?"

"You had the oddest expression on your face. What on earth were you thinking about?"

He was saved from coming up with a lie by the arrival of their host. Al Morgan pulled a chair up next to Nicki and sat down.

"How are you doing?" the gray-haired man said as he took Nicki's free hand in his.

She smiled. "I'm great."

Al studied her. "We've been doing some work with various metal alloys. It's all hush-hush stuff for the government, but it will have industrial applications. I was wondering—''

Nicki cut him off with a quick shake of her head. ''You're a sweetie for thinking of me, Al, but no.''

''Hear me out,'' he told her. ''We're talking very strong but extremely lightweight. You'd barely know they were there.''

''Braces are still braces.''

''But you'd be walking.''

Her smile was patient. ''The two-legged thing isn't all it's cracked up to be. Believe me, I've tried it.'' She released his hand and tapped his knee. ''Walking is what you know and I appreciate that you want that kind of freedom for me. But shuffling along in braces is slow and awkward.''

Al didn't look convinced. ''There are medical advances every day.''

''I agree and I have a doctor who keeps on top of that sort of thing. I trust her completely, but despite miracles, some things can't be healed. I learned that when I broke my legs.'' She smiled ruefully. ''The left one was so bad, even one of the ski patrol rescue guys passed out when he saw the bones sticking out. There was no way the bones could heal correctly. Walking was still a possibility because my right leg would be okay.''

She paused. Zane knew the story, knew how she'd struggled all those years ago. She'd been fourteen when her world had crashed in on her.

''Then I got a bone infection,'' she continued. ''It took months to heal and when it did, the bones in my right leg had been weakened to the point where they could never support my weight.''

''With physical therapy—'' Al started.

Nicki cut him off. "With physical therapy I can use braces. I can be upright and so what? It's hard work, not to mention painful. In my chair, I'm completely mobile."

"She's hell on wheels," Zane told Al. "Trust me—I've been run over."

She smiled at him. "Only when you're getting on my nerves." She turned back to Al. "I *can* walk with braces and a walker, I choose not to. A wheelchair beats the step-drag thing in my book."

Al didn't look convinced but he nodded. "If I can change your mind," he said.

"You can't."

She changed the subject to how his oldest daughter was doing at college. When Al was called away to look after his other guests, Zane touched her arm.

"Are you okay with him interfering?"

"Sure. He's doing it because he cares about me." She smiled. "I like that in a man."

Zane had always admired Nicki's courage and temperament. He found himself wanting to say that *he* cared, too.

"If he brings it up again, I'll go into more detail," she said. "Al sees me now, years after the accident. But if he'd been around when it happened, he would understand how far I've come."

She sipped her champagne. "Back then I would have agreed with him. I was determined to walk again, no matter how difficult it was or how much it hurt. When my parents bought me my first wheelchair, I saw it as a defeat. No way I was going to give in. Then one day I sat in it and I was amazed at how lightweight it was and how easily I could move around. Once I figured out I could outrun anyone and be involved in sports, I never looked back.''

Typical, he thought proudly. Nicki wasn't a quitter. ''Do you still have braces?''

''Sure, but I rarely use them. A friend from college got married and I was a bridesmaid. I used the braces so I could stand up with the rest of the wedding party, but I didn't try walking down the aisle in them. Back in high school and college I would take them to dances so I could shuffle around the floor with my date.'' She grinned. ''Sometimes I let the guys take them off. That always got them really excited.''

Young men unbuckling cool metal from her smooth, warm thighs? He could understand the attraction.

He pretended shock. ''You let them feel you up?''

''Of course.''

''Did your mother know?''

She rolled her eyes. ''Someone with your dating history is in no position to be judgmental. Besides, my prom date didn't get much more than a quick feel. I'm guessing your prom date offered you a chance to score.''

He shook his head. ''I didn't go to my prom. I was in a high school boot camp, paying my debt to society.''

''You're kidding? What had you done?''

He shrugged. ''Got caught in stolen truck with a few dozen TVs that didn't belong to me.''

''No way.''

''I was a wild kid.''

She leaned close. ''Okay, start at the beginning and talk slowly. I want details.''

"No way." He held up his glass. "I'd have to be a whole lot more drunk than this to spill that story."

She raised her arm to flag a waiter. He caught her hand and pulled it down.

"I'm driving, Nicki. One's my limit."

"How annoying. I'm going to have to lure you to my place then, with plans to get you drunk and worm the truth out of you."

He considered all the possibilities that went along with that and knew he should back off. Nicki was a friend—he didn't want that to change. Still he found himself agreeing to her plan, and anticipating the event.

Chapter Four

"You're going to have to invite me in," Zane said as he pulled up in front of Nicki's house.

Refusing to give in to the sudden fluttering in her chest, Nicki pretended a casualness that she didn't feel. "And that reason would be what?"

He grinned. In the dimness of the SUV, the only light came from the streetlamp. She was able to see the outline of Zane's face and the flash of his white teeth.

"You promised to get me drunk. Besides, it's barely ten-thirty. I have a reputation to think of. What would my neighbors say if I pulled in this early on a Friday night?"

"Of course," she murmured. "Your reputation."

There was no reason to refuse his request, she thought humorously. He didn't know about her out-of-control hormones. Nor was he likely to feel trapped if she had a brain hiccup and suddenly made a pass at him. No, the worst that could happen would be unfulfilled expectations on her part and Lord knew she'd been living with those forever.

"Far be it from me to ruin your stellar reputation," she said easily. "Come on in."

He turned off the engine and pocketed the keys. After collecting her wheelchair from the rear, he brought it around to the passenger side and locked the wheels. Then he opened her door and scooped her into his arms.

"Great perfume," he said as he settled her onto the chair's seat.

She could say the same thing except she knew Zane wasn't wearing a scent. That delicious fragrance she inhaled whenever they were close was nothing more than the man himself.

"Want a drink?" she asked when they were in the one-story house.

"Nothing alcoholic."

She tossed her purse onto the narrow table by the front door and wheeled into the living room. "There's an assortment of sodas and juices in the refrigerator. Help yourself."

"You want anything?"

"No thanks."

Zane sidetracked down the short hallway into the modified kitchen. She shifted restlessly in her chair, not sure what to do with herself. Or with him.

She glanced around at the clutter-free living room. She wasn't neat by nature, but she'd long ago learned that dropping items on the floor meant maneuvering around them later. Rather than turning her life into an obstacle course, she'd learned to tidy as she went.

The pale green walls picked up color from the striped green sofa. She'd picked the scaled-down piece of furniture because the firm back and arms allowed her to brace herself when she moved from her chair to the sofa. She'd placed a tall table behind the couch, rather than in front, and used floor lamps for light. There weren't any rugs to impede her progress, but she'd used prints, cushions and stackable tables to provide spots of color and warmth.

Zane returned from the kitchen with a can of soda in his hand. Instead of flopping down on the sofa, he crossed to her DVD collection and flipped through the movies.

"There's not enough death here," he complained as he held up a DVD with a picture of a couple on the front. "Too many chick flicks."

"Maybe because I *am* a chick."

He frowned. "Seriously, Nicki, there's not a decent car chase in the bunch."

"Amazingly enough, I didn't buy the movies for you."

"You can't tell me Brad enjoys these."

She shook her head. "You know his name is Boyd and *I* know you know, so why do you insist on pretending you can't remember?"

He blinked at her, his face an expression of innocence. "Know what?"

She sighed. "Fine. Be difficult. But I'll have you

know that Boyd enjoys romantic comedies as much as I do.''

Zane snorted. ''He's lying.''

''He is not. He likes the kissing.''

Zane walked to the table behind the sofa and set down his drink. ''Yeah, the kissing is okay, but the rest of it is boring.''

As he spoke, he bent over her and pulled her from her chair to the couch. Nicki didn't have time to protest, not that she was sure she would have. She liked sitting somewhere other than her chair, although she usually preferred to get there by her own power. Still, she couldn't complain about a few seconds spent in Zane's strong embrace.

He settled next to her and reached for the remote. ''You have cable, right?''

''Of course.''

''Maybe there's a game on.''

''Wouldn't that be special,'' she muttered.

He glanced at her. ''What's wrong? You're into sports.''

''I know.''

She enjoyed a good football or baseball game as much as the next person, but didn't Zane want to pay attention to her instead of a bunch of sweaty guys?

Obviously not, she thought as he flipped through over a hundred channels in less than two minutes. Note to self—this was not a real date and if she allowed herself to forget that, she was going to get her feelings hurt.

On his second round through the channels he

stopped on a familiar scene with Tom Cruise. It took her a second to recognize the movie *Top Gun*.

She laughed. "Okay, so this is the perfect movie, right? Planes, death, macho moments and kissing."

He chuckled. "You're right. Something for everyone."

He angled toward her and reached for his drink. After taking a swallow, he put the can back, but left his arm up on the back of the sofa.

His fingers were less than an inch from her shoulder. The second she realized that, she became painfully aware of how close they were sitting, of how she could feel him breathing. Tension crackled. Unfortunately it was all on her side. She doubted he was the least bit aware of her.

She told herself to pay attention to the movie. Tom and Kelly were having a heated argument, which meant the good parts weren't that far away. But she found her gaze being drawn back to the man sitting next to her. To his strong profile and the stubborn set of his jaw. To the long, dark lashes and the scar at the corner of his mouth.

"You're not watching the movie," he said as he tugged gently on her hair. "You'll miss the kiss."

She knew he was right, but she couldn't turn away. Zane was right there...close enough to touch. What would happen if she did something? Would he be shocked? Embarrassed? Would he let her down gently or would an answering desire flare in his eyes? Had he ever thought of her as something other than his friend?

There was only one way to find out, but Nicki

didn't think she had the guts. Yeah it was a new century and women were equals and all that but she was just plain scared. If Zane rejected her, it would change their relationship. Was she willing to risk not being his friend anymore?

The last question was easy to answer. She wasn't. So she looked at the screen and did her best to ignore Zane.

The scene shifted, the music swelled and the screen filled with the two lovers. Nicki allowed herself to get lost in the moment and forget about her own needs.

"Movie kisses are the best," she murmured without thinking. "Sometimes better than the real thing."

Zane had been drinking and he nearly choked. "Then Brad has been doing it all wrong."

She looked at him. "Boyd does it just fine. That's not the point. Movie kisses are often highly romantic. That's important. Not that you know much about romance."

He set down his drink. "I know plenty about bodies and that's what kissing involves."

"It's not just a function, like sneezing. It can be spiritual. The mind, the body, the heart are all engaged."

"You think too much."

"You don't think enough."

"Maybe not, but I sure as hell know how to kiss."

Nicki opened her mouth to shoot off some snappy retort when Zane suddenly shifted toward her. Before she could stop gasping like a fish, he wrapped his arms around her, pulled her closed and lowered his head.

She had just enough time to clamp her lips shut when he kissed her. A for real, skin on skin, bodies pressing, heat generating oh-my-is-this-really-happening kiss.

It was heaven. It was five kinds of wonderful and if she died right this second, her life would end on a really high note.

He pressed his mouth against hers with a firmness that spoke of confidence and authority, but with enough gentleness for her to know that he wanted to share, not just take. His scent surrounded her, allowing her to get lost in the moment as she breathed in the essence of the man.

His lips brushed against hers, exploring, teasing, before settling in place. She was still caught up in the wonder of what exactly was happening when he touched the tip of his tongue to her lower lip.

Heat exploded inside. Funny how that tiny point of contact could make her body go up in flames. She was aware of her breasts, her legs and that suddenly wet and swollen place between her thighs. She wanted Zane with a desperation that made her catch her breath. She supposed it came from fantasizing about him for so long...not to mention close contact with a man who knew how to excite a woman.

He traced the curve of her lower lip in a slow, delicious movement that made her mouth part. When he slipped inside and lightly stroked her tongue with his, her entire body clenched. Then he angled his head and deepened the kiss.

He touched and tasted and explored all of her. With each movement of the dance, she found herself melting into a puddle of desire. She didn't want to stop him—if anything she wanted to beg him to kiss her forever. But even if she'd wanted to put the brakes on, she was incapable of speech or movement or breath. She could only feel and savor those feelings.

His hands rested against her back. As the kiss continued, he began to slide them up and down her back. Strong fingers stroked against her. When he dipped lower and cupped her hip with his palm, she pressed into the contact.

She ached everywhere. The wanting grew until it was all she could think about. Need spun through her like a tornado; powerful, all-encompassing, overwhelming.

He shifted slightly and broke their kiss. Before she could protest, he pressed his mouth to her jaw, then along her neck. Hot tingles shot through her. At the same time he slipped his hand from her hip to her waist, then higher still. Anticipation made her cling to him. She dug her fingers into the tight, honed muscles of his shoulders and arms.

More. She needed more.

He pressed an openmouthed kiss to the sensitive skin just below her collarbone at the same time his hand closed over her breast. She sucked in a breath as his gentle touch soothed her aching flesh. His thumb brushed against her nipple and she gasped as fire jolted through her. Exquisite pleasure joined the out-of-control need. Between her legs, she melted, swelling, readying, wanting.

What had started as a simple kiss turned into something more. While Nicki wanted to lose herself in the moment, a persistent voice in her head screamed a single question over and over.

"What on earth are you doing?"

Did she want to be sensible and stop this? Did she want to ask Zane if he knew what he was doing? Not "did he know he was making love?" but "did he know he was doing it with *her?*" Never once in two years of friendship had he ever hinted that he saw her as someone other than a buddy. So why was he suddenly acting as if he knew she was a woman? And did she really want to know?

As if sensing her internal confusion, he sat up and stared at her. Passion darkened his eyes to the color of midnight. His mouth was damp and swollen, his hair slightly mussed. He looked so good that had he been a magazine ad, she would have assumed he'd been digitally enhanced.

The sound of a jet taking off cut through the silence. Zane turned, grabbed the remote and turned off the movie. Then he moved his hand from her breast and rubbed his thumb across her lower lip.

"Still think movie kissing is better than the real thing?" he asked softly.

Despite her questions and uncertainty, she smiled. "No. Doing is better than watching."

"Told you." He put his hand on her leg, then groaned softly. "You're not wearing panty hose. I noticed when I lifted you into the SUV. It's been driving me crazy."

Wow. Really? Did he mean that? "You try putting them on while sitting down. It's a pain."

He stroked her thigh. "I'm not a panty hose kind of guy."

She chuckled. "How awkward things would be if you were."

He didn't smile. Instead his already serious expression turned intense. "I didn't plan this Nicki. I don't make moves on women involved with other guys."

Other guys? Oh. "Boyd?"

"Yeah."

"I'm not..." She cleared her throat. Discussing this was difficult enough without the distraction of his hand moving up and down her thigh. "We haven't... That is to say things never got this far with him."

Zane's eyebrows lifted slightly. "If you tell me that you were willing and he held back I'm going to have to nominate him for stupid guy of the year."

The compliment delighted her. "I'm not sure either of us were interested."

"So I'm not trespassing?"

She shook her head, then nearly fell over from shock. They were talking about this whole thing as if they were going to keep going. As if it hadn't all just ended with a kiss.

Before she could ask, not even sure she wanted to know, Zane pressed his mouth to hers again. The kiss was long, slow, deep and impossible to resist. She surrendered to the feelings surging through her, to the taste and scent of him, to the hands roaming over her back and sides. When he slipped them up her ribs to her breasts, she could only breathe her pleasure.

He cupped her curves, then gently stroked her nipples with his fingers. She thrust her chest forward, silently begging for more.

When he responded by moving away, she moaned in protest. Against her mouth, he smiled.

"Impatient, aren't you?" he murmured. "I'm not going anywhere."

When he reached behind her, she understood his intentions and shifted so he could more easily reach the zipper of her dress. He pulled it down and slipped the silky fabric from her shoulders.

"Better," he whispered when he'd dragged the material to her waist. Expert fingers unfastened her bra.

She had a brief moment of concern, wondering if he would find her more modest charms interesting, but when he lowered his head and pressed an open-mouthed kiss to her already sensitized flesh she found she didn't care about anything but making sure he never stopped.

He licked her breast, then drew her nipple into his mouth. While his hand mimicked the movements on her other breast, she dug her fingers first into his shoulders and then ran them through his hair.

"Zane," she breathed.

Wanting filled her. The intensity of her reaction should have frightened her but thinking about it took a level of rational thought she no longer possessed. She squirmed to get closer, then pressed herself against him. He was aroused. She could feel his hardness against her hip. Unable to stop herself, she dropped her arm to her side and reached between them so she could touch him there. At the first brush of her fingers, he swore and stiffened.

When he raised his head the fire in his eyes had been dampened slightly by questions.

"Nicki?"

She pressed her lips together, not sure what he wanted to hear and what she wanted to say.

"I want you," he breathed. "If you're waiting for me to be sensible, hell's going to freeze over first. But I'll listen if you tell me to stop."

Stop? Was he kidding? She smiled, then brushed her fingers against his cheek.

"I would like it very much if you would stay."

Zane hadn't realized he'd been holding his breath until he released it. He hadn't planned to start kissing Nicki and he'd never intended for things to go this far. Had he thought it through, he would have assumed she would slap his face and toss him out on his butt. Yet if the warmth of her smile, not to mention her sensual reaction was anything to go by, she was more than interested.

He was smart enough not to question his good fortune, or risk the mood by considering the consequences. Instead he returned his mouth to her breast, while trying to stay focused enough to consider logistics.

He knew she wasn't a virgin. They'd talked about their dates enough over the past couple of years for him to know that while she was particular about who she invited into her bed, she did sometimes issue the invitation. He also knew that despite the lack of strength in her legs, she could feel everything.

He had a brief debate about moving things to the

bedroom or continuing them right here, and decided the sofa would work just fine.

That decided, he closed his mind to everything but the pleasure in touching her, pleasing her, and brought his hand up to her breast.

She tasted sweet. The flavor of her lips, her mouth, her skin all lingered on his tongue like fine wine. As he licked her tight nipple and felt her body shiver in response, he focused on the feel of her warm skin and how soft she was.

He brushed his fingers against her nipple, then gently teased it with his thumb. Her hands stirred restlessly along his back. Her nails scratched erotically. Heat swirled between them, enchanting his senses, making him want more.

He'd been hard since ten seconds into the first kiss and was getting harder by the second. The trick was going to be staying in control.

While he continued to lick and suck her breasts, he worked the bottom of her dress toward her waist. It was a dirty job, he thought humorously as he was forced to slide his hands against the silky smoothness of her thighs, but he was man enough to see the task through to the end. When there was nothing between himself and paradise but a pair of very skimpy bikini panties, he raised his head from her chest and shifted until he knelt on the floor.

Nicki opened her eyes and smiled at him. "Is this the part where you promise to be my devoted slave for the rest of your life?"

He smiled. "Would you like that?"

"Maybe. What duties come with that sort of servitude?"

He put his hands on her hips and eased her into a half-seated half-lying position. "I guess I'd have to be responsible for your sexual satisfaction."

As he spoke he pressed a kiss to the inside of her right knee. Thin scar lines crisscrossed her skin. He followed the trail they made all the way up her thigh.

She sighed. "I guess you deserve a tryout."

"Did I say I was applying?"

She raised her eyebrows. "Your position would say you were."

"Yours would say you wanted me to."

Her green eyes darkened. "You're right."

Their gazes locked. Blood heated and surged. It was all he could do to keep from unfastening his slacks, ripping off her panties and plunging home. But he'd given up one-sided sex about the time of his nineteenth birthday. These days he wanted his partner arriving at the finish line along with him. Which meant he had to get control.

Watching her watch him, he moved his hands up to her hips and hooked his fingers around her panties. Moving slowly, deliberately, he drew the scrap of silk down, down, down until he could peel it away. When she was bare, and still watching, he moved close and parted the slick, swollen folds of her feminine flesh. Then he opened his mouth and tasted her.

Paradise, he thought with the first flick of his tongue. His mind split neatly in two with one half wanting her climaxing so he could take his own release. The other half urged him to wait, to hold back, so he could taste and tease and pleasure her long into the night.

She groaned low in her throat and lightly touched his head. "I can't believe how good that is," she whispered. She pulled her knees back toward her chest. "Oh, Zane."

If was as if he could read her mind, Nicki thought hazily. Maybe he could. That was the only explanation for how he knew to go faster, then slower. He touched her with an attention to detail that left her unable to do anything but respond.

Within a minute, she was shaking. Within two she was panting, begging and on the verge of climaxing. Within three minutes...

Tension grew and grew until there was nothing in Nicki's world but the pleasure he created with his mouth and tongue and the ache filling her. She strained toward him, urging both of them on and found herself caught up in an orgasm that ripped through her like a hurricane.

Tossed, tumbled, set free and finally settling back onto the sofa, she needed a second to catch her breath. When she resurfaced, she found Zane staring at her intently. Need tightened his features, but smugness curved at the corners of his mouth.

"Not bad," she murmured.

"You're welcome to write a response card," he teased. "All compliments welcome."

She would have plenty of those. She couldn't remember the last time she'd been able to let go so easily. Even several minutes after the fact, tremors rippled through her body. Maybe because although he'd pleasured her, he still hadn't claimed her.

She tugged on the sleeve of his shirt. "One of us is a little too formally dressed."

She saw she didn't have to ask him twice. The words had barely formed before he went to work on his shirt. His shoes, socks, slacks and boxer shorts followed until he was naked and very, very ready.

He bent over her, moving her gently, positioning her lower body so he could ease himself between her thighs. The sight of his arousal made her own need roar back to life and when he knelt on the sofa, she reached for him.

"Be in me," she whispered.

He surged forward, filling her, stretching her, making her cry out in pleasure. His gaze locked with hers, allowing her to watch him take her.

His breathing increased with each stroke. He groaned her name over and over. The pace quickened and she felt herself losing control. Contractions rippled through her, making her cling to him, urging him on. He plunged inside of her, taking her to the edge, then flinging her out into the cosmos where she lost herself into glorious release before finding her way back.

When they had both recovered enough to breathe normally, Zane raised his head and smiled at her.

That was it. He didn't say anything, he simply smiled. And she smiled back because this felt good—right. Something she would never have guessed.

Then he stood in all his naked glory, scooped her up into his arms and carried her into the bedroom.

When they were both under the covers he looped an arm around her and pulled her close.

"Good night, Nicki," he mumbled.

Good night? He was staying? He never stayed. She knew that for a fact. He made it a point to cut and run after he'd had his good time. A thousand questions filled her mind, but before she could ask even one, she heard the quiet sigh that indicated he'd already fallen asleep.

She shifted so that she could study him in the dim light. She lightly traced the shape of his jaw, then pushed a lock of dark hair off his forehead.

The questions could wait, she told herself. For now this was enough. More than enough. It was more than she'd ever thought she would have.

Sunlight made a brutal alarm clock, Nicki thought the next morning when she opened her eyes and instantly had to squint. She started to turn to find out what time it was only to realize she was pinned under a strong, warm, heavy arm.

At that same moment, she realized she was naked, and that Zane was in her bed. Oh, and in case that wasn't enough, they'd made love. Not just the one time on her sofa, but also later. Here. In her bed.

Second thoughts arrived and they brought friends. What had she been thinking? Making love with Zane? Was she insane? Wasn't it bad enough that she had a completely foolish crush on him? Did she have to go and make it worse by bonding through intimate physical contact?

"I'm second cousin to the moron twins," she murmured, wishing she could simply duck and run. Unfortunately escape wasn't going to be that easy.

Her wheelchair was still in the living room. There weren't even any braces close by. Which meant she had the choice of waiting for Zane to bring her the chair or she could roll out of bed and drag her naked self across the hardwood floor. Given the two choices, she decided to wait.

Unfortunately there was the pressing problem of embarrassment, regrets and a rapidly filling bladder.

"Morning, good-looking."

She turned toward the voice and saw Zane was awake. Awake and smiling, which she couldn't believe. Like he was happy. Like they hadn't just made a huge mistake.

She offered a tight-lipped smile of her own. "Would you please get my chair and my bathrobe?"

"Sure thing."

He dropped a kiss on her nose, then rose. Once standing, he stretched his arms toward the ceiling. Apparently the naked thing bothered her a whole lot more than it bothered him. Of course his body was damn near perfect, so why would he care if she was looking? And look she did. At the lean muscles, at the dusting of hair on his chest and legs, at the shape and size of his maleness, impressive even at rest.

When he turned to leave the room, she admired the curve of his rear and the way his legs moved so easily.

He returned with her chair. While he was in the closet getting her robe, she pushed herself into a sitting position. After putting on her robe, she started to move into the chair. Zane lifted her into place.

"I can do it myself," she snapped.

He stepped back and raised his eyebrows. "I always thought you were a morning person."

"I am." She usually was. But this morning she felt out of sorts. Everything was confusing and more than a little scary.

"Come on," he said, jerking his head toward the bathroom. "Let's take a shower."

She couldn't believe it. "Together?"

"Sure. It's a great way to start the day. You wash my back…" His voice trailed off as he winked.

Oddly enough the suggestion made her more sad than annoyed. Her body went on instant alert at the thought of her up close and naked with Zane. But even as she considered the possibility, the logistics involved doused her like a face full of cold water.

Getting in the shower was more of a production for her than most people. She remained seated, she had special hold-bars and nonskid surfaces. Not the least bit sexy or appealing. She would imagine that Zane had pictured something along the lines of her up against a wall while he moved in and out of her, and that was so not going to happen.

"I have a lot to do today," she said at last. "If you want to shower, that's fine. There's a guest bathroom down the hall."

What she really meant was a regular bathroom. One that hadn't been modified for her personal use.

His dark gaze never left her face. For a second she would have sworn she saw a flicker of hurt, but she dismissed the possibility and told herself he was as anxious to leave as she was to have him gone.

The thought tightened her throat. Everything was different. In one night, two years of friendship had been materially changed and she wasn't sure she liked the differences. She felt awkward and vulnerable. And Zane…well, she didn't know what he was feeling.

"No problem, Nicki," he said and headed for the door. "I'll get out of your way."

She watched him walk out of the bedroom. Far more quickly than she could have imagined, he was back—fully dressed and acting as if nothing strange had happened.

"I'll call you later," he said as he bent down and lightly kissed her cheek.

She nodded because what she really wanted to say was that he didn't have to bother, but she didn't know how to speak the words without them coming out wrong. She wasn't trying to be mean. Instead she wanted to tell Zane that he wasn't obligated in any way. At least not to her.

He gave her a quick smile, a wave and then he was gone. As she sat in her chair, in her bedroom and stared at her rumpled bed, she heard footsteps, then the sound of the front door opening and closing.

Part of her wanted to call him back. Part of her never wanted to see him again, and most of her wanted to go back in time and rethink the decision to spend the night with him.

They were lovers now, at least they had been. But for how long, and what would happen when that part of their relationship ended? Zane didn't do long-term and she didn't do affairs. There was also the matter of their friendship and what impact this would have on that. Not to mention her feelings. How much had their intimacy caused her to bond with him?

Nicki sighed and headed for the bathroom. This situation was going to take a whole lot more than a shower and a couple of hours to figure out, but right now she didn't have anything close to a better plan.

Chapter Five

Neither the shower nor time helped. By noon Nicki was restless and practically itching to do something— but what? Maybe it didn't matter, she thought as she tried to concentrate on sorting laundry. Maybe she just needed to occupy her mind so she didn't have so much time to think. Because she'd been thinking all morning and all she'd achieved was to give herself a massive headache as she wondered why on earth she'd slept with Zane.

Last night had been amazing. More than amazing. It wasn't just that Zane knew his way around a woman's body, although that was nice, too. It was that despite her limitations, she never once felt less than normal. He'd found positions that allowed her to move and be a part of things. He'd taken her sugges- tions and incorporated them into their lovemaking in such a way that she'd been able to lose herself in the experience of being with him.

He'd made her feel good—not just with an assortment of orgasms but by laughing with her and treating her like his best friend with whom he just happened to be having sex.

Just thinking about their night together made her long for him. Which terrified her. Longing wasn't allowed. Longing implied a level of connection on her side of things that went way beyond her crush. She'd known from almost the first moment she'd met him that Zane wasn't a forever kind of guy and her long-term goals included marriage and a family. If he wasn't going to be a part of that, it was really dumb to waste her heart on him.

But could she choose who she cared about? It had been relatively easy to keep her feelings in check before, but what about now? And why didn't Zane want more than a series of short-term flings? What was it about him or his past that caused him to walk away? And why on earth had she slept with him?

"Stop it," she commanded herself. All this circular reasoning wasn't accomplishing anything. Maybe she should go for a drive or something.

She rolled toward the front of the house where she kept her purse and her keys. As she passed through the living room, the phone rang.

Nicki froze. While there were several people who *could* be calling, she knew exactly who was on the other end of the line. The certainty made her hesitate before picking up the receiver. What finally got her moving was the reminder that she'd long ago learned there was no point in avoiding the inevitable. Putting it off only made it worse.

"Hello?"

"Hey, gorgeous," Zane said, sounding cheerful and friendly. "How you doing?"

"I'm okay," she said cautiously.

"Just okay? You should be wonderful. Last night was pretty great. I do have all that practice."

His comments were no more outrageous than usual. In the context of their friendship, her move was to make some witty response that firmly put him in his place. Or if she was to go into lover mode, she would agree that last night had been wonderful and so was he. But she couldn't seem to find any words and when she did, her mouth wasn't working right.

He stepped into the silence. "I thought I'd swing by later and we'd go out."

That single sentence was almost as stunning as the previous night. "What?"

"Catch a movie, have some dinner. You'll need to drive because I had to return Ashley's SUV, but I'm tolerant of your feminine inadequacies behind the wheel so don't sweat it."

Dinner and a movie? Like a date? Was he kidding?

"I don't understand," she told him.

He sighed theatrically. "I'll speak more slowly then," he said as he demonstrated by leaving a noticeable pause between the words. "It's the weekend. We should go out and have fun."

Nicki closed her eyes. Her chest felt tight and she wasn't sure why. Suddenly everything hurt, most especially her heart. If she gave into the feeling, she could be in tears in less than a minute.

He was asking her out. She didn't know what it meant, but there was no way she trusted him. Or what he was doing. She wanted to yell at him. She wanted to yell at herself. Neither made sense.

"Nicki?"

"I'm here," she murmured.

"What's going on?"

"Nothing."

Everything. He wanted to make plans. She thought of her laundry piles and the fact that she had to call Boyd and break things off officially. Not that he was going to be heartbroken. Based on how he'd been canceling dates lately, he'd been having some second thoughts of his own.

But with Boyd there had been possibilities. Promise. And with Zane there was nothing.

"I can't," she told him. "I have things I need to get done. But thanks for asking."

Then, before he could say anything else, she hung up and started to cry.

Zane stared at the phone and wondered what the hell had just happened. Obviously Nicki was upset, but why? She'd enjoyed last night. Every time he'd reached for her, she'd been wet, willing and doing her own fair share of grabbing. They'd made love into the hours before dawn, then had slept entwined. He didn't usually like to spend the night, but with Nicki it had felt right. There hadn't been any sense of being trapped by expectations.

So what was up with her this morning? His first instinct was to go see her and demand an explanation. But he was unsure of his welcome—something that had never happened before with Nicki. He didn't like it.

Restlessness stirred him. He wanted to run. Literally.

He moved through the living room to the bedroom and emerged a couple of minutes later in shorts, running shoes and an old T-shirt. A minutes after that, he was out the door, so he wasn't around when the phone began to ring.

Nicki knew she was slime. Maybe even worse than that. Whatever had happened between Zane and herself, she didn't have the right to blow him off when he called. She'd been raised better than that and certainly considered herself a nicer person than she'd shown by her behavior. More importantly, he was her friend and she'd treated him badly. An apology was in order, which explained why she was now navigating a part of the city that made her uncomfortable…the marina.

Zane lived on a houseboat in a neighborhood made famous by the movie *Sleepless in Seattle*. His houseboat sat along a dock in Lake Union. She'd been to the two-story home a couple of times before and each time had been reminded that this area was not wheelchair-friendly.

The ramp down to the dock had crossbars every couple of feet. She understood the purpose was to keep people from slipping when the ramp was wet—something that happened frequently in the Seattle rain. But each bump meant slow going for her. The railing looking sturdy enough, but was at such a height that if she fell out of her wheelchair, she would slip between the rails and fall into the chilly lake below.

Once she reached boat level, there was the dock

movement to contend with, followed by an impossibly high step entrance onto Zane's houseboat. Which meant she couldn't roll up to the door and knock. Instead she was forced to pause on the dock and call him from her cell phone.

"It's me," she said when he picked up. "I'm right outside your front door."

Seconds later the door in question opened and Zane stepped out into the afternoon sunlight.

He looked good, she thought as her stomach clenched and her heart rate increased. Too good. Clean shaven, freshly showered and just a little wary. She couldn't blame him for the latter, even though it made her feel like slime.

"What's up?" he asked as he approached.

She managed a smile. "The four most horrible words known to your gender. We have to talk."

He grinned. "I can handle it."

She was glad one of them could.

He stepped onto the dock and scooped her into his arms. "You didn't have to come here," he said. "I know you don't feel comfortable in the houseboat. I would have come to you."

"That would negate the power of my groveling."

They were close enough that she could see his individual eyelashes and feel the beat of his heart. Her body reacted to the nearness by heating up while her mind seemed in danger of shutting down.

He looked at her. "Are you groveling?" he asked.

"I plan to."

"Lucky me. I'll be in the front row."

He set her on the sofa, then went outside to bring in her wheelchair. When he returned, he moved a few pieces of furniture out of the way and rolled up a rug.

While he worked, she glanced around at the small, tidy space. The beauty of houseboats was life on the water with more room than on a traditional boat. Huge windows offered impressive views of the lake and the rest of the marina. Low bench seats hugged the walls, providing extra space for guests and storage underneath.

The color palette—teals, blues and greens, with gold and burgundy accents—had been provided by the previous owner with a flare for decorating. While Nicki enjoyed the elegant touches, such as the refurbished nineteenth-century light fixture over the dining room table and the parquet floor, she sensed that Zane would have been just as happy in a house of beige.

When he put her back in her wheelchair and took a seat in a club chair, she knew it was show time. Funny how in her van on the way over she'd known exactly what she was going to say and now her mind was a complete blank.

"I called you back but you were out," she said by way of a stall.

"I went for a run."

She nodded and tried to figure out what he was thinking. Did he seem wary, or was that just guilt on her part?

She sucked in a breath and cut to the chase. "I'm sorry I hung up on you. I was…upset."

He frowned. "Why?"

"Because of last night…and this morning."

"Didn't you want us to make love?"

How like him to go for the heart of the matter with one simple question. Had she wanted them to make love?

"Yes and no."

"That makes it clear."

He spoke with just enough amusement that she knew he wasn't mad. Relief filled her, making it easier to tell him the truth.

"Zane, we're friends," she said earnestly.

"I know. I like us being friends."

"Me, too. Our relationship is important to me and I don't want to mess it up."

"I agree. But what does that have to do with last night?"

"Everything. Friends don't sleep together."

"Why not?"

She stared at him. "You have got to be kidding. There are a dozen reasons why not."

"Give me three."

Of course her mind went blank that instant.

"Because."

"That's not a good reason," he told her.

She already knew that, but it was the only reason she could think of that she could tell him. She couldn't say if they slept together, he would start to matter too much. Her crush could turn into something else. Something she didn't want to think about because one of these days she was going to lick the Zane problem and actually fall in love with a guy who would want to love her back.

"I liked things the way they were," she said instead.

He looked genuinely baffled. "But the sex was great."

"Agreed."

"Then why wouldn't you want to keep doing it?"

Did he have to be such a *guy?* "Because eventually you won't want to have sex with me. Then what? I don't think we can end things as lovers and still be friends. You don't do long-term and I don't do affairs. So we're at an impasse. Honestly, as good as it was last night, I would rather be friends than lovers.''

He rose to his feet and crossed to the window. She watched his movements, as always taking pleasure in his body. He was graceful and athletic in everything he did. She knew he took his mobility for granted, as most people did.

He turned to face her. ''But we...'' He shook his head and swore. ''You're being sensible.''

Relief settled over her. He might protest, but he didn't fundamentally disagree. She'd been afraid that he would think the sex was more important than their friendship, which would have been fabulous in the moment, but tragic over time. As friends, they could be there for each other indefinitely, but as lovers, there was a ticking clock until things ended.

''I don't agree with this,'' he told her.

''Yes, you do.''

His mouth twisted. ''I don't like it, then.''

''I'm with you on that. Last night was amazing and I would be more than happy to jump back into bed with you right this second.''

His expression turned predatory as he took a single step toward her. She held up a hand to stop him.

''You know it's far better to just be friends. You have plenty of lovers, Zane, do you really need another one?''

''You don't have any.''

Good point, and something she didn't want to think about. ''I'll get one, eventually. Until then, can't we have things the way they were before?''

He shrugged. ''Sure. If that's what you really want.''

''It is.''

But oddly enough, she didn't sound convinced, and when he continued to look at her with his dark eyes, she was suddenly aware of the subtle movements of the houseboat. They made her wonder what it would be like to make love on the water, with the sounds of the lake all around and the sunlight illuminating Zane's perfect body.

''You're thinking about it,'' he said.

''I'm not,'' she lied, then knew it was foolish to deny the truth. ''Okay, maybe a little, but that doesn't matter. Maturity is important. Think of this as building character.''

He didn't say anything. Instead he continued to watch her, which made her wonder if he was going to ignore her request that things go back to what they had always been. If Zane swept her up in his arms and carried her to his bedroom, there was very little she could do to stop him. So she would have to give in and it wouldn't be her fault.

Don't go there, a voice in her head screamed. Making love with Zane again would put her too close to falling in love and then what? She would have completely fallen for him and he would be itching to walk away. Better to ache with wanting than bleed from a broken heart.

''What is this supposed to be?'' Nicki asked the next afternoon as she stared at the array of large boxes loosely connected by twist ties and staples. Ashley Ritter laughed at the question.

''It's a carnival booth. Can't you tell? For Maggie's

school. They're having a fall festival as a fund-raiser. I volunteered to decorate one of them and when this was delivered, Jeff instantly went into macho 'I can build better.' It was all I could do to keep him out of the garage. He would do anything for his daughter.''

Nicki smiled at the softness and love in Ashley's voice and did her best not to feel envious of her friend's happy marriage. Not that Nicki would want Jeff for herself, but someone who adored her with Jeff's devotion to his family would be nice.

''He's been making me crazy for the past couple of days,'' Ashley continued, ''which is why I sent him off to the movies with the kids. I knew there was no way this was going to get finished otherwise.'' She smiled. ''You're so sweet to offer to help me with it.''

''How could I resist?'' Nicki teased as she picked up a length of crepe paper. Besides, it beat being at home trying not to think about Zane, while being unable to think about anything else.

''How are you feeling?'' she asked, nodding at her friend's still flat midsection.

''Okay.'' Ashley plugged in the glue gun and dumped a bag of cut-out leaves in fall colors onto the kitchen table. ''The all-day sickness is fading, thank goodness. The bad news is once it's gone completely I'll start eating for twenty and pile on the pounds. As I'm a couple of years older this time, I'm guessing they won't come off as quickly as they did with Michael.''

''You look great,'' Nicki told her friend.

Ashley laughed. ''Your gentle spirit is one of the reasons I love you.''

Nicki rolled her eyes. ''I'm many things, but I

don't know that gentle would make the list.'' She thought of how she'd freaked out the previous morning with Zane. Crazy fit. Or in need of serious counseling. Or a brain transplant. Maybe that would help her get over the man.

Ashley handed her the glue gun and the paper leaves. ''Want to talk about it?''

Nicki stared at her. ''Talk about what?''

Ashley unrolled crepe paper. ''Whatever has you so unsettled. You've been jumpy since you arrived.''

Nicki spent three seconds figuring out if she was going to tell her friend the truth, then knew there was no way she could lie.

She glanced around the spacious black-and-white kitchen before realizing that looking for an escape route wasn't going to help her, either. Then she took a deep breath and came clean.

''You know Zane and I were together at the party Friday night,'' she began.

Ashley nodded. ''I was stunned at first, but excited. You've been in love with him since the second you laid eyes on him.''

''It's a crush,'' Nicki corrected.

''If you say so,'' Ashley said, not sounding convinced.

Nicki ignored that. She was already in so much trouble, she didn't need to go looking for more.

''After he drove me home, he came inside. We were talking about movies and he complained that all I have in my DVD collection is romantic comedies.''

Ashley leaned toward her. ''Would you quit stalling and cut to the chase. What happened?''

Nicki shifted in her chair. ''We started kissing and one thing led to the other and he spent the night.''

"Are you talking about sex?" Ashley asked, her voice loud and high-pitched. "I can't believe it. You had sex with Zane?"

Nicki set the glue gun down, then covered her face with her hands. "I know. I can't believe it, either."

"Sex?"

She straightened. "Could you stop saying the *s* word, please?"

Ashley laughed. "I don't know. I'm stunned. More than stunned. In complete shock. How was it? I mean I'm sure Zane has more than enough experience to make things go smoothly, but I know it can be awkward for you the first time."

Nicki nodded. "Usually it is. I have to explain what I can feel or what I can or can't do, but not with Zane. He and I have talked about my legs enough that he knew most of that stuff already." She sighed as she recalled their close encounter on the sofa.

"He was perfect. Passionate, exciting, gentle. I forgot about everything but being with him. It was great."

Ashley's hazel eyes widened. "Wow."

"That pretty much describes it."

"So what's the problem? Why are you obviously unhappy and why on earth are you here, instead of out doing the wild thing with him?"

That was the more difficult question. "I don't know," she admitted. "I guess the truth is I'm scared."

Ashley's humor faded and she touched Nicki's hand. "Of caring too much?"

Nicki nodded. "Zane doesn't take any romantic relationship seriously. There's no reason to think I

would be any different. I decided I would rather be
his full-time friend than his part-time lover.''

''I understand your reasoning, but between your
feelings for him and things being great in bed, that
can't have been easy. Weren't you tempted to at least
try things out with him?''

''Sort of,'' Nicki murmured. ''Okay, yes. I was
very tempted. But it would be crazy.''

''It wouldn't be boring,'' Ashley said.

''You're not encouraging me to pursue an affair
with Zane are you?''

''Of course not,'' Ashley said, but Nicki wasn't
convinced.

''Do you know how much I could be hurt? If I fell
in love with him, it would be devastating.''

''I know. You made the sensible choice.''

''Why don't I believe you think that?''

Ashley shrugged. ''Because you might not believe
it yourself. You've had it bad for Zane from day one
and you've yet to get over him. You finally get him
into bed only to find out it's even better than you
thought. Of course you're ambivalent. Who wouldn't
be?''

Nicki tried to smile. ''You're supposed to reinforce
my decision, not make me question it.''

''Sorry. I don't mean to make you more confused.
You were right. Why would you want to have an
ongoing physical relationship with the only man to
make you practically glow when you could continue
to be friends and die a slow death of frustration from
wanting him?''

''He would get tired of me and dump me.''

''You don't know that.''

''He's never done anything else with a woman.''

"He's never slept with you before."

Nicki opened her mouth and closed it. "You're not helping. Friends is better. Trust me. I've thought this through. I'm making the sensible decision. It will be better for both of us."

"If you say so."

"I do."

Nicki knew she was right. The sensible path was always the right one. And in time, she would even start to believe that herself.

Chapter Six

Monday morning Zane arrived at the office at his usual time. He could have gotten there about three hours earlier because he hadn't slept much the night before, but he'd been too busy pacing the length of his houseboat to come into the office.

Everything was completely screwed up and even though he could say why, he didn't understand what was wrong. He hadn't planned on sleeping with Nicki. He'd asked her to the party because neither of them had a date and they enjoyed each other's company. They always had fun together. He figured the party would be more of the same.

As for picking her up and treating her like she was his date—he'd liked that. He enjoyed the company of beautiful women and when they were also funny and challenging like Nicki, how was he supposed to resist?

She'd blown him away with her combination of elegance, humor and style. Not to mention how she'd made him feel in bed.

Lying down together meant her legs weren't an issue. There was no body weight to support and she'd moved with a sensuality that had left him breathless. He wouldn't have cared if she'd needed things to go differently, but what had excited him had been her abandon because *he'd* wanted her with a desperation that had stunned him.

He'd thought she wanted him as well. But she'd sure as hell been quick to put the brakes on. One minutes they'd been lovers, the next…friends.

He walked into his office and turned on his computer. But his mind was still on Nicki. On what had happened and what she'd said. Of course they had to be friends, he thought irritably. She was his best friend. And in theory staying away from each other made sense. But he didn't want to stay away from her and he hated that she was disconnected enough to see the logic in playing it safe. He wanted her to be so swept away by passion that she couldn't think.

"Not working out?" Jeff asked as he paused in the doorway to Zane's office.

Zane shook his head. "I ran this weekend."

Jeff nodded and left. Zane sank into his chair. He'd done more than run. He'd doubled his usual distance, pushing himself until his body screamed for him to stop. He'd run until he'd been so exhausted he'd been sure he wouldn't be able to think…but he had. He'd thought about Nicki.

"Mr. Sabotini has decided it would be better for him to make the trip here," Jeff said at the staff meeting Monday afternoon. He glanced at Zane, then at Nicki. "Sorry guys. Looks like your trip to Italy is off."

Zane said something noncommittal while Nicki could only sigh in relief. The last thing she needed right now was long-distance traveling with Zane. She didn't want to be in the same room with him, let alone trapped on a plane with him for several hours.

Just sitting across the conference table from him was enough to get her blood pressure into the danger zone. It had been bad enough before when she could only wonder what it would be like to be the center of his universe, if only for a few hours. Now that she knew the unique combination of pleasure and unwavering attention, she found herself unable to think of anything else. Not even work.

"Once he finalizes his travel plans," Jeff continued, "we'll set up a meeting. He thinks it's going to be in L.A. or Chicago."

"Either works," Zane said.

"Fine," Nicki agreed.

Jeff frowned slightly, then shrugged and continued with the meeting.

There were bodyguard staff to assign, new clients to research and ongoing operations to be updated. Nicki followed along, making notes on the items that she would have to get involved with. Brenda, Jeff's assistant, made another stab at being allowed to test for a field operative. Without thinking, Nicki glanced at Zane and smiled.

He was already looking at her. Their gazes locked but that friendly connection quickly spiraled to something much more. She felt the heat from clear across the large table. Need flared inside of her. She wanted to be anywhere but here, as long as she was alone with Zane. She wanted to be naked, begging, pulling him closer, having him suck in his breath as he lost himself in her body.

Startled by the intensity of the flashback, she jerked in her seat and turned away. Embarrassment heated her cheeks. Work, she told herself. She was physically at work and she needed to keep her brain there as well.

When the meeting wrapped up, Nicki stayed in place until the room cleared. It was her habit, and usually Zane kept her company. But today he was one of the first people out the door, while Jeff remained seated at the head of the table. A knot formed in her stomach when he got up and closed the door behind the last person.

''What's up, Nicki?'' he asked when they were alone. ''You're not yourself.''

She thought about asking who he imagined her to be but didn't think he would appreciate the humor. ''I'm okay.''

Jeff came around and took the chair next to her, angling so he faced her. His expression was kind.

''There was a lot of tension between you and Zane,'' he said. ''Normally I can't get the two of you to shut up and pay attention. Today you weren't talking.''

She ducked her head. Obviously Ashley had chosen not to tell her husband about what had happened between Nicki and Zane. While Nicki appreciated her friend keeping the confidence, she didn't know what to say to Jeff about the situation.

''We'll be fine,'' she murmured at last.

''Why don't I believe that?''

She looked at him. "I won't let any personal issues interfere with my work."

He smiled. "I know. You're too good at what you do. That's not why we're talking. You're important to the company, but you're also a friend."

She liked Jeff, but being friends with him was very different from being friends with Zane. Despite Jeff's blond good looks, she'd never once thought of him as anything other than her boss and Ashley's husband.

"Have you two had a fight?" he asked.

She shook her head. Not at all. Instead of arguing, they'd gotten too friendly and now Nicki didn't know how to return things to their normal footing.

"Please don't worry, Jeff."

"Hard not to, but I'll do my best." He paused, then smiled at her. "Did I ever tell you that my first wife's name was Nicole?"

"No. Does she look like me, too?"

"Not even close. You're nothing like her in any way. After we split up, I learned that some things can't be changed and some things can't be undone. My door is always open, Nicki, and I want to be there for you. My advice about all of this is to remind you that you can only do what's right for yourself. You can't control anyone else."

She knew he was talking about Zane, but she had no idea what he was trying to say. Was he warning her away from a personal relationship with his partner or telling her to go for it? Not that it mattered. She'd already made her decision. She was going to do everything she could to turn back time so that one glorious night was forgotten and she and Zane could be friends again. That was the best course of action for both of them.

She only hoped it wouldn't take a miracle.

* * *

Zane left his office and headed for Nicki's. He was willing to accept that things were going to be awkward between them for the first couple of days, but she was taking things too far.

He rounded the corner and stalked into her office. She looked up as he entered, saw his expression and frowned.

"What's wrong?" she asked.

He dropped the copy of the e-mail on her desk. "This."

She glanced at the paper, then at him. "You can't make it?"

"No. You asked if I was still coming with you."

Her green eyes darkened with confusion. "Yes, I know. I sent the e-mail."

He paced the length of her office, pausing as he turned to glare at her. "That's my point," he told her. "You asked. Dammit, Nicki, why are you doing this?"

"What?"

"Acting as if everything has changed. I've been helping you with your demonstrations on the first Monday of the month for over a year. Why would this be different?"

She pulled off her headset and leaned back in her chair. "I know. I'm sorry. It's just…"

He knew what it was. They'd become lovers and in her mind, that had changed everything. It had changed things for him, too, but he'd been willing to work through those differences, while spending some quality time in her bed. She didn't want that.

"You want us to be friends and nothing more," he

said. "I respect that. So why are you the one acting as if we barely know each other?"

Color stained her cheeks. "I don't mean to do that. I feel awkward around you."

Awkward? "Why?"

"Because."

There was an answer. He pulled up the chair in front of her desk and dropped into the seat. She felt uncomfortable and probably wished the whole thing hadn't happened while he... He wished they'd never stopped being together. It wasn't just that he wanted to keep making love with Nicki, although he did. But what he really missed was the connection.

As soon as the thought formed, he pushed it away. No connections, he reminded himself. No bonding, no caring, beyond what they already had. That was his rule and he'd lived by it for a long time.

"It's the naked thing," she said without looking at him. "Weird things happen to women when they get naked with a guy."

"Things other than sex?"

She glanced at him and smiled. "You're making fun of me."

"Only a little."

She rested her forearms on the desk. "I know it was really great and everything, but I can't help wishing we'd never done that. Don't you?"

He couldn't answer the question, not honestly. Nor did he allow himself to have an emotional reaction to her statement. She had regrets. Fine. He could live with that.

"I'll be there tonight," he said stiffly. "We'll pretend Friday never happened."

She winced. "I didn't mean that, exactly. I had a really good time."

"Sure." Why not? He was pretty decent in bed. He'd received enough compliments to have faith in his abilities. "I gotta get going," he said as he stood.

"Zane, wait. Let's have dinner tonight. After the demonstration."

He looked at her beautiful face, at the cascade of red hair that fell over her shoulders. He'd buried his hands in her hair as he'd made love with her. He'd touched her and kissed her and laughed with her. He'd wanted her, when he wasn't supposed to allow himself much more than scratching an itch.

He thought about the phone message he'd listened to on his voice mail. The call he'd yet to return.

"I can't make it," he told her. "Heather left me a message. She's in town for a couple of days and asked me to meet her for dinner. Maybe another time."

Nicki's smile never wavered. "No problem. See you tonight."

He waved and left the room.

Nicki watched him go. She managed to maintain her composure for all of twenty-seven seconds, then she slumped in her seat and had to blink back tears.

"I refuse to cry over him," she whispered fiercely. "Dammit, I'm the one who told him we were going to be friends and I meant it. So I refuse to care that he's having dinner with Heather."

Oh, but it hurt, she thought, feeling more miserable by the second. It hurt so much she could barely breathe.

Her phone rang and she considered not answering it. Then she reminded herself that she couldn't let her personal life interfere with her job.

"This is Nicki," she said after she clicked on her headset.

"Hey, it's me." Ashley's gentle voice came over the phone line. "I wanted to see how you're doing."

Her friend's concern nearly undid her, but she managed to keep from bursting into tears.

"I'm okay."

Ashley sighed. "You're lying. I can hear it from ten miles away."

Nicki swallowed. "It's just so stupid. I mean Zane wanted us to hang out and do stuff and I'm the one who said no and now things are weird, only I know they're not weird because we're not hanging out but because we had sex and I told him I wished we'd never done it and I think that hurt his feelings and now he's having dinner with Heather."

"Impressive," her friend said. "I think you got that out in one breath."

Nicki sniffed. "You're making fun of me."

"Not really. I'm trying to lighten the situation. Is it working?"

"A little."

"I am sorry, if that helps. And I've been worried about you."

"I appreciate that. You also didn't say anything to Jeff."

"How do you know?"

"He stayed to talk to me after the staff meeting because he'd noticed something was wrong between me and Zane. But he obviously didn't know what."

Ashley chuckled. "I thought the information would be more than he would want to know. So I kept quiet." She exhaled. "*Are* you having second thoughts about being only friends?"

"No." Nicki knew the danger inherent in wanting more with Zane. She would get her heart broken and getting over him would take forever. She had other plans for her life.

"I know I made the right decision. But why is he having dinner with Heather?"

"Because he's not having dinner with you?"

"Maybe." Nicki wasn't sure. "I wouldn't mind so much if she was like all the others, but Heather is smarter. And she and Zane went out for a really long time. What if she wants to start things up with him?"

"Why do you care?" Ashley asked.

"Good question. I shouldn't, huh?"

"If you're his friend, you should be thrilled he's found someone."

Nicki wanted to say she was happy, only that would be lying, too. "I want to scratch her eyes out."

"I sort of figured that."

Nicki closed her eyes. "Does that mean I've already fallen for him?"

"You don't want to know what I think," Ashley told her.

"Probably because I already know the answer. If I'm feeling jealous of Heather, it could be too late."

"I'm not the one saying that."

"You don't have to. I can figure it out for myself."

Had she fallen for Zane? And if she had, what was she going to do about it?

"There has to be a solution," Nicki said.

"You could always try the 'fake it until you make it' school of thought. Act as if everything is fine until it is fine."

"You think that will work?"

"Sure."

But Ashley's bright, cheerful tone didn't fool Nicki. Her friend thought she was already in trouble and that the worse was yet to come. Nicki hoped she was wrong.

"Whoever is attacking you isn't going to expect you to fight back," Nicki said that evening as she addressed the small group of people in the community center.

She grinned as she spoke. "Surprise is your friend and I'm going teach you how to take the element of surprise one step further."

Zane listened to the familiar speech. He and Nicki had been traveling around the Seattle-Tacoma area for over a year, talking about staying safe and self-defense for those with a physical disability. She talked tactics and demonstrated moves, while his job was to be the bad guy.

Tonight's group included a couple of elderly women in wheelchairs, an older man who used a walker and two kids in wheelchairs. There was also a teenage boy in a wheelchair, but he wasn't part of the group. Instead he sat at the far end of the room and stared out into the twilight.

Zane returned his attention to Nicki. For the demonstration, she'd dressed in sweatpants and a loose T-shirt. Her hair was pulled back into a braid. Whatever had bothered her earlier in the day seemed to have faded, leaving her looking happy and gorgeous.

He, on the other hand, felt restless. He hadn't seen Heather in nearly a year and he knew he should be anticipating their evening together. Instead he found himself wishing he was going out with Nicki instead.

Really dumb, Rankin, he told himself. She's not interested.

Nicki finished with her lecture and he took his position up behind her. She'd placed a large handbag on her lap. At her signal, he strolled toward her, then reached down for the bag.

As he grabbed it, she screamed and tugged on the opposite end of the handle. Even though he knew it was coming, he was still surprised by her sudden release. He stumbled slightly. She took advantage of his moment of being off balance and slammed into him.

Nicki might weigh about a hundred and twenty pounds, but she could generate some force with her wheelchair. As he stumbled back, she kept moving forward. When he tried to sidestep, she banged into him again, this time not so dead on. He two-stepped, turned and found himself slipping.

While he struggled to regain his balance, she grabbed the purse and took off across the room. He knew her top speed beat his and didn't bother trying to chase her down. The audience applauded.

They went through the exercise a second time, this time moving slowly, with Nicki explaining why she moved in, how to throw him off balance and when to run. He attacked her from behind, then tried to pull her out of her chair.

The latter move was the only one to have a chance of success, but he wasn't always able to dislodge her. He could physically lift her out of her chair, but that required getting in close and Nicki had several self-defense moves to make that a poor choice.

The entire lecture and demonstration took about ninety minutes. By the end, she'd won over the group.

One of the things Zane liked best about working with her on these demonstrations was the change in attitude of those attending. At the beginning of the meeting, they were self-conscious and already convinced they were simply victims on wheels. Nicki showed them what was possible and allowed them to believe in themselves.

After the meeting ended, there was time for coffee and conversation. Zane glanced at his watch. It was about seven-thirty and he was due to meet Heather at eight. But instead of leaving, he collected a cup and chatted with those attending.

"Zane, good to see you," a white-haired woman said as she joined him.

"Betty." He smiled at the center's director. "We have a full house."

"Always. You and Nicki are some of our most popular speakers." Betty patted his arm. "She gives them hope."

He followed her gaze and saw Nicki in the corner with the teenaged boy in the wheelchair. He was no longer solemn and isolated. Instead he watched Nicki intently as she showed him how to balance on two wheels and spin around.

"Nothing his mother will want him to learn," Betty said dryly, "but probably the best thing for his spirit."

"She's good at that."

One of the older ladies wheeled over to him and smiled. "You and your wife did a wonderful job," she said. "She's a lovely young woman and you're a very special man."

Zane nodded and thanked her. Ever since he and Nicki had started doing this together, he'd had at least a dozen people come up and talk about his "wife." He'd given up correcting them—it took too long and they were always disappointed.

Betty waited until the woman had left, then shook her head. "You might as well go ahead and propose, Zane. It seems to be your destiny."

He chuckled, then excused himself and made his way to Nicki.

"I'm heading out," he said.

She frowned. "I bumped into you harder than I meant to earlier. Did I bruise you?"

He raised his eyebrows. "I'm a macho guy. Girls don't bruise me."

"Girls in metal wheelchairs can leave a lasting impression."

"I'm fine," he told her. It was his cue to leave, but somehow he couldn't make his feet move.

She poked him with her foot. "Zane, it's getting late. Heather's waiting."

He stared at her green eyes, at her easy smile and the relaxed pose of her body. Had they made their way back to the friendship she wanted? Wasn't it for the best if they did?

Comments from little old ladies aside, they weren't married and they weren't going to be. He had no claim on her. But if they were friends…

She was important to him. So important that he was going to walk away before he did something stupid.

"See you tomorrow," he said.

"Have fun."

He turned and walked out of the community center. As he put the key in the driver's door of his car, he had a last thought about canceling dinner with Heather and going out with Nicki instead.

No, he told himself as he slid onto the seat. She was right. No more dinners, no more nights into mornings. Not for the reasons she thought, not because he couldn't do a relationship but because he chose not to. He'd killed the last woman he'd loved. He wouldn't ever risk that again. Not with anyone and certainly not with Nicki.

Chapter Seven

By Thursday Nicki knew she had to get over the whole Heather thing or she was going to collapse from lack of sleep. She'd fretted for the past three nights, knowing Zane was out with the woman and possibly staying until dawn. Telling herself she'd been the one to send him away didn't make her feel any better. She'd vacillated between polishing her resumé, picking up the phone to invite him back into her bed and signing up for a dating service.

She'd settled on a couple of nights with too much ice cream and a good cry over a romantic movie.

At three the previous morning, she decided to give herself a virtual slap upside the head. If that didn't work, then she was going to get serious about finding a different job. If being around Zane made her miserable, then it was time to move on.

Feeling mature and in control, she drove to the

building about ten miles from the main office where she would help train new bodyguard recruits. She always enjoyed these exercises and looked forward to the action. Her confident mood lasted until she pulled into the parking lot and saw Zane waiting by the back entrance. At the sight of his dark good looks her heart fluttered, her thighs heated and her stomach began to hula. So much for being in control.

He waited until she'd lowered herself to the ground and wheeled away from her van, then he strolled over and handed her a take-out coffee from Starbucks.

"Brenda's bringing doughnuts," he said. "I told her to make sure there were plenty of glazed."

"Thanks." She took the coffee and sipped. "Exactly how I like it. Very thoughtful."

He shrugged. "I'm a thoughtful kind of guy. How was your evening?"

"Uneventful."

She'd finally met with Boyd and had officially ended their rapidly dying relationship.

"Yours?" she asked.

"Take-out pizza and baseball."

"I don't remember Heather liking sports."

"I didn't see Heather. She went back to Dallas."

"Oh."

Nicki told herself the information was mildly interesting at best, but that didn't stop her from feeling relieved. Zane bringing her coffee and waiting to escort her inside reminded her of the old days. B.N.—before naked. Were they finally on their way to returning to normal?

"You ready for today?" he asked as they moved into the building.

"I think so."

He glanced at her white shirt. "You sure you want to wear that?"

She grinned. "It's more dramatic."

"If you say so."

By ten that morning, the six new recruits were seated in front of computer terminals and learning about the basics of hacking.

"Time is always an issue," Nicki said from her place at the front of the classroom. "Even with our sophisticated password programs, you're unlikely to get into a hard drive in seconds. If the information is vital and you have a clear way out, sometimes it's simply easier to take the damn thing with you."

Several of the students laughed.

She smiled. "Especially if it's a laptop. But the real trick is when you need to get information without the person knowing you were there. Obviously then a little thievery is not going to work."

There was another appreciative chuckle.

"Okay, let me explain the basic premise of the program," she continued. "Any password is nothing more than a string of characters, be they letters or numbers or symbols. If you can—"

The classroom doors burst open. Four people tore into the room and aimed rifles at the students.

"Nobody move," one of the men yelled. "Nobody breathe. Stay in your seats."

Nicki wheeled toward the man talking. "What do you want?"

He aimed his gun at her chest. "Shut up, sweetheart, and no one gets hurts."

"Take out your wallets and cash," a woman said. "Slowly."

Nicki glanced at her purse on the floor. ''I have to move to get mine,'' she said.

The man swung around and shot out a light. One of the students screamed.

''This is ridiculous,'' Nicki told the man, her voice loud and heated. ''You can't just burst in here and rob us. I won't—''

But she didn't get to say what she wouldn't do. The man returned his attention to her, dropped the rifle to his side, pulled out a handgun and shot her.

Nicki felt the thud against her chest, then spreading wetness. She glanced down and saw a red stain blossoming against the front of her blouse.

The sight of it was enough to make her woozy. She glanced back to the man, then leaned forward and toppled onto the ground. There was screaming and the sound of tussling. Then footsteps as the group grabbed purses and wallets and fled.

The lights went out. There was more yelling and screaming, then the lights flipped back on and Nicki heard Zane's voice.

''Stay calm, people,'' he said as he crouched next to her.

She raised her head. ''I hit my elbow when I fell.''

He helped her into a sitting position, then lifted her back into her chair. ''You okay?''

She rubbed the spot. ''Sure. I'll have a bruise, but that's the price one pays for drama.''

He chuckled. ''You always make it look so real when you tumble to the floor.''

''I don't have that far to go, so it's easier for me to relax.''

He looked at her blouse and winced. ''Is that going to wash out?''

"It always does."

Nicki unbuttoned the blouse and shrugged out of it, then pulled off the fake blood pack and the plastic protecting her lightweight sweater underneath. After stuffing it all in a bag, she glanced at the students.

They looked shell-shocked and more than a little stunned. Good. They were supposed to be.

"Ready?" Zane asked.

She nodded and wheeled back to her computer terminal.

"All right, people," he said taking his place in front of the class. "Take a deep breath and get focused. I want each of you to think about what just happened. Yes, it was unexpected, but attacks usually are. You have to stay alert in every circumstance. Now Nicki is going to take you through a series of questions. The purpose is to figure out what you think you saw versus what really happened." He glanced at her. "Go for it."

She nodded and typed a few keys. The large screen behind her illuminated as it displayed what was on her laptop. She scrolled to the beginning of the list of questions.

"We'll take these one at a time. Go through the questions and write down your answers. Be as thorough as possible. Impressions, feelings and details. When you're finished we'll compare notes, then we'll go through the scenario again, this time more slowly." She grinned. "And while I'll get shot a second time, there won't be any blood."

The students chuckled, then went to work. As they wrote Zane moved close, then crouched in front of her.

"Lunch," he said. "Mexican. You're buying."

"But I was just shot."

"Right. And you're so excited to still be alive, you want to buy me lunch."

She grinned and nodded. The last of the tension inside of her faded away. After stumbling through some awkward moments, she and Zane were back on their regular footing. They were friends who cared, who teased and that was how she wanted things to stay. Better to be his friend in the long-term than his lover for a couple of weeks. Now she simply had to work on getting over her crush so she could move on with her life.

Two weeks later Nicki pulled her luggage to the back of the van and prepared to lower both it and herself to the ground.

"We need to talk about a ramp," she said to Zane as he waited for her to come to a stop.

"How about some kind of hoist?" he asked. "We could load you like a bag of rice."

She rolled her eyes. "I'm in a wheelchair, Zane. You could be a bit more delicate."

He considered her statement then shook his head. "Where's the fun in that?"

"Oh, yeah. This is a real thrill a minute."

She rolled off the van's ramp and let Zane take possession of her luggage. While she raised the ramp and locked her van, he carried the suitcase to the private company jet they would use to get to Los Angeles.

After pocketing her keys, she headed for the gleaming white plane. When she'd locked her wheels, Zane swept her into his arms and carried her up the stairs.

"Watch my head," she told him. "Last time you crashed me into the doorway."

"I did not. Your hair might have lightly grazed the edge—"

She cut him off with a laugh. "I nearly had a concussion."

"If your mother knew how much you lied to me, she would be desperately disappointed."

"If she knew you'd nearly killed her only child, she'd slap you silly."

His only response was a shake of his head as he stepped into the plane.

Nicki knew Zane was right—her hair had barely brushed against the door frame, but she wanted the distraction of them teasing so she wouldn't notice how good he looked...or smelled. There was also the thrill of being in his arms as he carried her into the plane and set her carefully in a plush leather seat.

"Oh, to be rich," she murmured as she stroked the smooth covering. "Were these upscale seats standard or did you pay extra?"

He sat across from her and stretched out his legs. "When you drop twelve million on a plane, they throw in the leather."

"How nice."

The copilot walked back. "You two ready?"

Zane looked at Nicki who nodded. "I'm braced for air flight," she said.

"Then we'll head out."

"Are you going to do the in-flight announcements?" she asked Zane.

"Keep your seat belt fastened or I'll toss you off the plane."

She wrinkled her nose. "You need to work on your people skills."

"All my skills are in excellent working order. That's why I'm going to meet with this very important client. I'll dazzle him."

"I didn't think guys were your style."

"I'm ignoring you," he told her.

"Maybe I should do the dazzling," she said.

"Did you bring your braces?" he asked. "Then you'd be upright and he could pinch your butt."

"That *does* sound thrilling." She pretended to consider the opportunity. "Maybe later."

"Speaking of fun, how's Brad?"

She'd wondered if he would get around to asking about him. "Boyd is probably fine, but I don't know for sure. We aren't seeing each other."

She braced herself for teasing or questions, but there wasn't, either. Instead he slumped down in his seat.

"His loss," he said quietly.

The plane taxied to the end of the runway, then turned and moved forward. When they were airborne, the captain's voice came on over the loud speaker and gave them an estimated flying time.

"We'll be landing at the Santa Monica airport. The limo is already confirmed."

"Limo?" Nicki raised her eyebrows. "How very upper class."

Zane tossed a magazine at her. "Quit acting as if all this is a surprise. We've used a limo before."

"I know but it's fun to tease you."

"Actually Mr. Sabotini is the one providing the limo, and we're staying in his hotel."

Nicki was surprised. "I've never met anyone who had his own hotel."

"I believe he's part owner in the chain. Don't get too excited. There's a Mrs. Sabotini."

"Bummer. How about sons?"

"The oldest is about sixteen."

"Hmm, for part ownership of a hotel chain, I could hang around for a couple of years until he comes of age."

Zane grimaced. "Not funny."

"Oh, sure. Because it's a woman showing interest in a younger man. But if you had an eighteen-year-old woman hovering around..."

He shook his head. "Too young. Despite your low opinion of me, I actually like to have conversations now and then."

Nicki sensed they were heading into dangerous territory. She didn't want to think about what had happened between Zane and herself, let alone talk about it. Time to change the subject.

"Mr. Sabotini seems to have gotten himself into a little bit of trouble," she said.

"Agreed. International banking can be difficult at best, but when he inadvertently financed some nasty business in the Middle East, all bets were off. There have been multiple death threats on him and his family. The police are involved, but he wants something extra. Which is where we come in. Coffee?"

"Sure."

While Zane walked to the small galley, Nicki leaned forward and grabbed his briefcase.

"Okay if I get out the files?" she asked.

"Help yourself."

She withdrew the thick folders on Mr. Sabotini,

then flipped open to the presentation Zane and Jeff had worked up.

"Is he going to agree to pull his kids from their school?" she asked.

"I have no idea, but if he doesn't, he's a fool," Zane said. "These people don't play around."

He returned with two cups of coffee and set one on the small table next to her seat.

"Jeff briefed you on the plan before we left, right?" he asked.

She nodded. "I think it will work, if our client cooperates."

"That's part of our job. To convince him that we're the right company and to remind him that cooperation on his part means staying alive."

The limo pulled up in front of an elegant white building just off Rodeo Drive. Nicki glanced around at the exclusive shops and familiar designer names.

This area wasn't exactly in her price range, she thought, but if there was some free time, she wouldn't mind looking around.

She studied the level sidewalks and wheelchair accessible curbs. At least she wouldn't be dependent on Zane to cart her from place to place. Unlike getting in and out of the limo. As they pulled up to the hotel, she waited patiently while he went around back and collected her wheelchair, then set it next to the rear door.

While she couldn't complain about his attentive service, she had to admit that she didn't like being dependent on him. Yes, being held in his arms got her hormones dancing, but that charming reaction didn't override the sense of being helpless and a bother. Nicki much preferred to make her own way in the world, which was why she'd designed her life so that was possible. Unfortunately situations during business travel weren't always within her control.

There was also the underlying uneasiness from their recent intimacy. She'd traveled with both Jeff and Zane, but always in the capacity of an employee and friend. Never as an ex-lover. She didn't want things to be different between them but she couldn't help sensing that they were.

"Ready?" Zane asked when she was settled in her chair.

She tucked her small handbag next to her hip and nodded. "What time is our meeting this afternoon?"

"Two. We have a couple of hours to get settled. Want to order room service for lunch?"

"That would be great."

She could use the extra time. While specially equipped handicapped rooms made travel easier, there were still problems that had to be worked through.

They approached the front desk. Nicki was pleased to see it was low. Most were so high, she couldn't see the person she was talking to. Either she had to go around to the end, or the person assisting her had to hang over the front.

"May I help you?" a young woman in a navy suit jacket asked.

"We have reservations." Zane gave their names.

The woman touched several keys on her computer keyboard, then raised her eyebrows. "Of course. You are both special guests of Mr. Sabotini. We are delighted to have you staying with us."

Nicki glanced around at the elegant decor of the spacious lobby. In this kind of place, everyone received excellent service. However as she and Zane were "special guests," she had a feeling they were going to be overwhelmed with attention. Not bad duty.

"If you'll sign the registration cards, please," the woman said.

Nicki took hers and glanced at it. "This doesn't say anything about the room being wheelchair friendly," she said. "I want to confirm that it is. I made the request last week."

The woman stiffened. "I'm aware of that, Ms. Beauman, but there isn't a handicapped room available. I'm so sorry. We're happy to upgrade you into something much nicer."

Nicki swallowed panic. "I don't want nicer," she said, keeping her voice calm. "I didn't ask for the room on a whim. As you can see, I use a wheelchair. I require the amenities that come with the room."

The woman nodded and picked up the phone. Zane initialed his form and passed it back.

Nicki held onto hers. Hotel rooms were not her friend. The walking areas were often narrow and littered with obstacles. The vanities were too high, the toilets a nightmare to get on and off of. She could never use the closets because the racks were well above her reach. Then there was the horror of a regular tub, which meant having to step over the side—something she couldn't do.

Looking distraught, the woman hung up. "I'm sorry, Ms. Beauman, but we only have two such rooms in the hotel. The first is occupied by a guest who also requires special amenities. The second had a pipe break and was flooded. It is currently under repair, but is not habitable at this time."

For the most part Nicki was able to ignore her condition. It simply existed and she lived her life, doing pretty much what she wanted. But every now and then circumstances conspired to make her life complicated. This was one of those times.

"A regular room won't work," Nicki said, trying not to panic. "My wheelchair won't fit between the pieces of furniture. There's no way I can step over a regular tub. Or use a closet. I can't reach that high. Even with my braces, I'd find the room a hazard."

Zane listened quietly. He'd never considered the difficulties Nicki experienced when she stepped out of her routine. For him, one hotel room was like another. But for her...

He thought about her house. The hardwood floors, the heavy furniture spaced far enough apart that she could easily wheel around it. He'd never used her private bathroom, but he didn't doubt it had been modified, just like her kitchen.

He knew they could change hotels. While he would normally suggest that, in this case there was the problem of their client.

"Give us a second," he told the clerk, then led Nicki away from the desk.

"What if I helped?" he asked. "It could be fun. You like bossing me around."

She shook her head. "There's no way I'm going to phone you every time I need to move around my room."

"I was thinking more along the lines of us sharing a suite. I'd be there to fetch and carry. You could just lie back and give orders."

She didn't smile, which he'd kind of hoped for, but her tension seemed to ease a little.

"You're not my servant."

"Agreed, but admit it. There have been times you'd like me as your slave."

One corner of her mouth quirked, then stilled.

"There are personal things involved, Zane. Things that are outside of the bounds of friendship."

He leaned close and lowered his voice. "Nicki, I've not only seen you naked, I've pretty much had my tongue and mouth on every inch of you. How many mysteries could there be?"

She shifted in her seat. "Okay, you might have a point there. But the whole idea makes me uncomfortable."

"I don't want that." He touched the back of her hand. "I'm happy to share a suite with you and do whatever needs doing. Under normal circumstances I wouldn't suggest it."

She sighed. "But Mr. Sabotini owns the hotel and he'll be offended if we stay somewhere else."

"Not if we tell him why."

She grimaced. "I don't think I want to have that conversation." She looked at him. "This could be very weird."

He winked. "Yeah, but I get to see you naked."

He waited for her remind him they were just friends and that nothing was going to happen. Instead she rubbed her hands against the wheels of her chair.

"I don't want you seeing me like that to change anything."

He stared at her, at her big green eyes and the slight quiver of her mouth. He'd seen Nicki gloating, laughing, angry and wild with passion, but he couldn't remember ever seeing her vulnerable before. Something inside of his chest tightened.

He leaned close and touched her cheek. "I have always admired you. Nothing abut that is going to change. I swear."

She swallowed. "If you're lying, I'll run you over."

He grinned. "It's a deal."

They returned to the front desk where the young woman was delighted to give them a large two bedroom suite. A bellman took up their luggage, and Zane and Nicki followed.

The suite was on a high floor, with huge windows and a north-facing view. Several Oriental rugs covered a marble floor. Sofas and chairs formed conversation groups, while a black lacquered table and chairs sat up on a dais by the window.

Nicki glanced around the room. "The rugs will have to go," she said.

The bellman pulled a small notepad out of his pocket and wrote down the instruction. "Anything else?" he asked.

She wheeled through the room and pointed to an end table, a small desk and two chairs. From there she went into the master bedroom.

Zane ducked into the second bedroom which was nice, but not nearly as opulent as the living area. He checked out the bathroom and bedroom, then walked into the master.

The bed was on a platform, but there was plenty of open floor space. He found Nicki in the bathroom. Again there was plenty of room for her to maneuver around. The large glass shower had a built in bench.

"I'll take the other bedroom," he said. "You'll be able to get around in this one."

She hesitated, as if she were going to protest, then nodded. "Thanks."

"No problem."

She had the bellman take up the small rugs in the bathroom, then returned to the living area.

Two men had already arrived and were removing the unwanted furniture. When they'd finished, Zane glanced at his watch.

"Let's order room service and then unpack," he said.

"Okay."

She picked a salad off the menu. Trying not to gag at the thought of lettuce for lunch, he ordered her meal, then got a burger for himself, with extra fries because he knew she would be stealing his. Then he carried her suitcase into the master bedroom and set it on the bed.

He'd already seen the closet so he knew there was no way she could reach up and hang her own clothes.

"Tell me what you want where," he said as he flipped open the top of the case.

She had him hang her two suits and blouses, then put lingerie, a nightgown and stockings in a drawer.

She didn't look at him as she spoke and he could tell she wasn't happy about the situation.

He dropped to his knees in front of her and took both her hands in his. "I don't know how to make this better for you," he said.

"That's not your job."

"Sure it is. We're friends." He squeezed her fingers. "Nicki, you're damned independent most of the time, which is all any of us ever get to say. Sometimes we need a little extra help."

"I know that in my head, but it still bugs me. I don't like you doing all this extra work."

"I know how you can repay me."

Her expression turned wary. "How?" she asked cautiously.

"Let me rub your panties all over my body."

She jerked her hands free of his. "That's too disgusting for words."

He grinned. "I'd let you watch."

"Don't even think about it."

Now that her good humor had been restored, he told her the truth.

"I think you're amazing," he said quietly. "You're smart, beautiful and not half-bad in bed."

She smiled. "Gee, thanks."

"None of that is about you being in the chair. I don't mind helping out. You'd take care of me if the tables were turned."

"I know, but they aren't. Nor are they likely to be."

"Next time I have the flu I'll call you over to fix me soup."

"Actually you'd have to come stay at my place."

"Even better." He winked. "You can give me lots of sponge baths."

She rolled her eyes. "Is everything about getting naked with you?"

"Pretty much."

"That is just so typical."

"Can I help it if women find me irresistible?"

"Not all women."

"Enough do."

He wanted to tell her that she was one of them but didn't want to hear her say she wasn't. After all, Nicki had been the one to put the brakes on their physical relationship, not him.

"Thanks," she said, squeezing his fingers. "For all of this. And for making it easy. Now why don't you go unpack before our lunch gets here? Did you order extra fries?"

"Of course."

"Good."

She smiled.

For a second they just looked at each other. Something hot and bright flared between them. Zane thought about leaning close and kissing her—for two reasons. Because he wanted to and because at that moment he knew she would kiss him back. But he didn't. There was a fragile peace between them that he didn't want to shatter. For reasons he couldn't explain, having Nicki need him was somehow more important than having Nicki want him.

Chapter Eight

"Nicole," Mr. Sabotini said at the end of their meeting. "I want your promise that you'll be serving as, how do you say, backup?"

She smiled. "I'll be there making sure they get it right."

"Excellent."

He took her hand and lightly kissed her knuckles. "You have impressed me."

Okay, so the man was smooth and probably only meant about thirty percent of what he said, but Nicki didn't care. She liked hearing the flattery and the compliments. After all, how often did an elegantly dressed Italian man stare adoringly at her? She couldn't think of a single incident.

"You've made the right choice with our firm," she said as she disentangled her hand. Flattery was one thing, but while Mr. Sabotini might not be thinking of his wife, Nicki was very clear on her existence.

Zane stood and collected their files. "I'll phone the office and have the contracts drawn up."

Mr. Sabotini rose. "I would like the team in place as soon as possible."

"We'll overnight the contracts. Once you sign them and provide the retainer, we'll move into place." Zane shook the man's hand. "Two of our best child-protection agents have just finished an assignment. They're already making arrangements to fly to Italy."

"Good. I worry about my boys." He smiled at Zane, then turned to her. "Nicole. You must tell me the next time you visit Italy."

"You'll be the first," she murmured, then wheeled toward the exit.

They left the spacious suite only two floors above their own and headed for the elevators.

"That went well," she said.

Zane chuckled. "Yeah. I want to say we sold him on our reputation and the quality of our bodyguards, but I think your legs were a good part of the appeal."

"He was being polite."

"He was drooling."

She smiled. "Mr. Sabotini likes women. As I was the only female in the room, I received all of his attention."

Zane shook his head. "Sorry kid, but you don't get off that easily. I think there could have been ten women in the room and he still would have focused on you. I couldn't decide if I should offer to leave you two alone or take him out back and beat the crap out of him."

She would love to think that Zane was jealous but her imagination wasn't that good. Their client's attention had been just the ego boost she needed and she refused to apologize for that.

They reached the elevator lobby, but instead of pushing the down button, Zane pushed up.

"Where are we going?" she asked.

"To the rooftop restaurant. I made reservations for us so we would have somewhere to celebrate."

"And if we hadn't closed the deal?"

"Hot dogs and beer."

She was still laughing when the elevator arrived.

The rooftop restaurant offered a gorgeous view. It was clear in Los Angeles, warm, with a soft breeze. To the west, the sun slipped toward the horizon.

She was shown to a table on the edge of the patio. Several tall potted trees provided privacy, while a tall gas heater stood by in case the evening became chilly.

The waiter had already whisked away a chair, so Nicki was able to glide into place. She placed her napkin on her lap then picked up the menu. Zane was still by the front podium, calling Jeff to let him know what happened.

"I told him we want a raise," he said as he approached a few minutes later. "And that we were brilliant. Mostly me, of course, but I gave you some of the credit."

"Gee, thanks."

"No problem." He pulled out a chair and sank down on the seat. "So what looks good?"

They discussed various menu choices, had a conversation with the waiter about wine, then picked entrées and a bottle of cabernet sauvignon.

"The only thing that would make this day any better would be you telling me you want me to run you a bath later,'' Zane said with a grin.

Nicki knew he was kidding, or at least teasing. And she really appreciated his help while they were staying at the hotel. But she couldn't help wishing—just for a second—that she didn't need it.

"What?" he asked, leaning toward her. "You got quiet and sad."

She shook her head. "I'm being silly."

"I'll be the judge of that."

She debated changing the subject versus telling the truth. Funny how of all the people she knew in the world, outside of her parents, he was the only one she could imagine confiding in.

"Sometimes the limitations get me down," she admitted. "I try not to go there and most of the time I succeed, but every now and then…" Her voice trailed off.

"Like when you have to maneuver through strange hotel rooms?"

"Yeah." She shrugged. "Plus I hate you seeing that I'm not perfect."

He grinned. "Nicki, I've never once thought of you as perfect, so this isn't a revelation for me."

She chuckled. "You know what I mean."

"I do. You're not in control and no one likes that. You weren't born this way. You can remember what it was like not to deal with the chair." He glanced around as if making sure they were alone. "If you ever repeat this, I'll deny saying it, but I think you're a hell of a woman."

The combination of sincerity and teasing nearly brought tears to her eyes. Trust Zane to get it exactly right.

"You always make me feel good about myself."

He nodded. "I'm a pretty spectacular guy. And modest."

"Especially modest." She touched his hand. "I could have used someone like you around when I first had my accident."

"You were what, fourteen?"

She nodded. "We were on a skiing vacation over the holidays. Neither of my parents had any family and before I was born they'd gotten in the habit of traveling over Christmas. When I came along, they kept up the tradition."

She smiled as she remembered how happy those trips had been. "No matter where we were, they always made Christmas special."

She'd been a miracle baby, born three days after her mother's fortieth birthday. Her mother had always joked that if she'd received Nicki for turning forty that she couldn't wait to see what fifty would bring.

"The resort had dug out a couple of trees that had been knocked over by high winds, but they hadn't gotten around to filling in the holes. Whatever signs they'd put out had disappeared. I came tearing down the mountain right into a ten-foot pit."

Zane winced. "That had to hurt."

"I don't know. I hit my head, so I was unconscious until we got to the hospital. By then I was in shock and spacing out. It took a couple of days and two surgeries before I knew what was going on."

The waiter appeared with their bottle of wine. While he opened it, someone else brought bread and their salads.

Zane tasted the wine and nodded his approval. When they were alone, he raised his glass to her.

"To staying strong," he said.

She nodded and sipped.

"After a few days my parents were told my left leg would never heal right. There were too many breaks and there was no way to put it all together. I was okay with that. I figured I could survive a limp."

Zane didn't think he would have survived the same experience with Nicki's faith in life and good spirits.

"Then you came down with the bone infection," he said.

"Exactly. That was tough. They had to open me up again, scrape stuff out. I was on so many antibiotics I practically glowed. My parents were frantic with worry."

"You pulled through."

"But the bone was weakened forever." She picked up her fork. "I went into physical therapy. Once there I learned I wouldn't be walking again. Not without braces and a walker. It was a real downtime. I thought…" She glanced at him, then away. "I really thought about killing myself."

"Makes sense."

She looked surprised. "But that's the easy way out."

"Nicki, you were what, fifteen? Your entire life had been shattered. Of course you'd think of ending it all. Who wouldn't?"

"I thought everyone else would be stronger than me. I've dealt with a lot of guilt over my plan." She smiled slightly. "I have to say being underage and in a wheelchair made the 'how' pretty difficult. Then one night while I was sitting alone in my room, I heard a voice."

He stared at her. "What kind?"

"I don't know. It was in my head. I'd never heard it before or since. It wasn't my voice or my folks. It wasn't anyone I knew. But it told me I was an idiot. I had parents who loved me, unlimited opportunity and if I ended my life over something as foolish as not being able to walk then I was too stupid to live anyway."

She shrugged. "I figured if I was hearing voices, I'd better listen."

Over the past couple of years he'd learned various details about her injuries and subsequent recovery, but he'd never heard this.

"What happened?" he asked.

"I made the decision to get over myself. I threw myself into physical therapy and went back to school. Once I figured out I could still play sports and have a life, I did the best I could and never looked back."

"Any more voices?"

"Not even one." She took a bite of her salad and chewed. "Once I accepted myself, I found all my friends were more than ready to accept me."

"I'll bet." He imagined a sixteen-year-old Nicki. "You broke hearts on a weekly basis."

"I don't know about that, but I did have boy-friends. I told you before that I wore my braces to the prom so I could slow dance."

He didn't want to think about that—about some high school senior carrying her out to the dance floor and holding her close.

Crazy to be jealous of a ghost, he told himself. Maybe if he didn't still want her, he wouldn't mind so much.

"You showed them all," he said. "Even your-self."

"I learned I'm a survivor. I think that's an important lesson."

He agreed. But Nicki had done more than survive. She'd thrived.

"Have you—"

But whatever he'd been about to say got lost when he looked up and saw her watching him. There was something in her eyes, something bright and hot and passionate.

Heat exploded inside of him. In less than two seconds he went from interested to hard. His chest tightened, his hands curled into fists and damn it all to hell, he couldn't seem to catch his breath.

"You said friends," he reminded her when he could finally speak.

"I know."

Her voice, more murmur than whisper, made him think of being naked with her. Of tangled sheets and soft cries and the thrill of pleasing her.

He wanted to tell her they couldn't do this. That he understood her reasons for wanting them to be only friends and he respected them. But he couldn't seem to say the words. Maybe he just didn't want to.

"I know I'm changing the rules," she said. "Is that okay?"

He managed a smile. "You think I'm going to tell you no?"

She smiled. "Then I guess we should get dinner to go."

It took a few minutes to settle things with the waiter and collect their take-out boxes. Nicki tried to keep her mind perfectly blank because if she thought too much about what she'd said, about what they were going to do, she would start to hyperventilate.

She knew this was crazy, that *she* was crazy. She had very logical, sensible reasons for keeping things on a "friend's only" footing with Zane. She didn't want to get her heart broken, she didn't want to lose him. She wanted to be free to fall for someone else and get started on her happily ever after. But she couldn't seem to not want him.

She'd just told him her deepest darkest secrets and instead of running for the hills, he'd looked at her as if she were his hero. How was she supposed to resist that? Plus he'd been so sweet about them sharing a room. He'd made jokes and gone out of his way to make her feel special and normal. That all combined with spending time alone with him had apparently undone her good intentions, leaving her little more than a liquid puddle of longing.

The elevator ride to their floor was short and silent. Nicki didn't know where to look and when her gaze accidentally landed on Zane's face, she nearly fainted at the desire she saw etched there. Whatever doubts she might have about the foolishness of her decision to make love with him again were overshadowed by the fact that he wanted her just as much as she wanted him.

When the elevator doors opened, they exited and moved directly to the suite. Zane already had the key out. He pushed opened the door and she entered. He was right behind her. She heard the slap of the take-out containers hitting a table, but she was already heading for the bedroom. As she rolled, she reached down and pulled off her shoes, while shrugging out of her suit jacket.

That's as far as she got. Zane caught up with her halfway across the bedroom and knelt in front of her wheelchair. Then his hands were on her face and he was kissing her with a desperation that made her heart break.

His warm, firm lips took as much as they offered. She tasted wine and a hint of the man himself.

At the first brush of his mouth, her breathing caught and she parted her lips for him instantly. When his tongue swept inside, touching her, teasing her, making her want with a force that should have terrified her, she ceased to need breath. As long as she had this man, as long as he touched her and allowed her to touch him, she would survive. This moment was enough. This world in which they were lovers was paradise.

"I want you," he breathed as he kissed her cheek, her nose, her forehead. He cupped her head and gazed into her eyes. "Nicki."

The sound of her name was as erotic as the most intimate touch. She shivered in anticipation of what was to come. Of how they would be together. She was already damp. She could feel the wetness on her panties. Her breasts had swollen, as had that most intimate part of her.

"Zane," she whispered as she ran her fingers down his cheeks.

He wrapped his arms around her and drew her out of the chair and onto his lap. Leaning up against an oversized chair, he cuddled her close and kissed her.

These were slow, deep kisses. Kisses of preparation and exploration. Waves of sensation crashed through her as she struggled to get closer and closer. If only she could crawl inside of him, everything would be all right.

He kept one arm around her. His other dropped to her lap where his hand began a lazy exploration of her legs. While he nibbled on the corner of her mouth, then sucked her lower lip, he tickled the inside of her knee and slowly began to drift up her thigh.

For her part, she explored his broad shoulders, then began to unbutton his shirt. She wanted to feel bare skin against her own. She wanted to make *his* breath catch as much as her own.

"So beautiful," he whispered as he rained kisses down her throat and across her collarbone. "So—"

The hand on her thigh froze. She felt a little jolt of her own as he crossed from the top of her stocking to skin.

He raised his head and looked at her. "What the hell are you wearing?"

She couldn't help smiling at his tone of outrage. "What I always wear when I have to put on stockings. A garter belt."

He swallowed, swore, then swallowed again. "You're kidding?"

She shook her head. "Have you ever tried putting on panty hose while seated in a wheelchair? It's just about impossible. I can't stand up and all the wiggling in the world isn't going to pull that waistband into place. I gave up years ago. Actually the whole stocking thing is the reason I prefer pants. But for business meetings, I'll put on thigh-high stockings and a garter belt."

Heat flared in his dark eyes. "You mean to tell me that every time I've been in a meeting with you and you've been in a skirt, you've had this on underneath?''

As he spoke he caressed her thigh and the garter belt clasp.

"Sure."

He groaned. "Thank God I didn't know."

She looked at him. "What's the big deal? It's just underwear."

"Nicki, it's a whole lot of things, but 'just underwear' isn't one of them."

He shifted onto his knees, then still holding her, stood and walked to the bed.

"I'll admit it's completely adolescent, but I have to see," he murmured as he placed her on the mattress and reached for the side zipper of her skirt.

The garment slipped off, and he stared at her. Nicki raised up on one elbow to see what all the fuss was about. To her the view was what it always was. Garter belt, panties and stockings.

"I don't get the big deal," she began, right as Zane bent over and pressed an openmouthed kiss to the top of her thigh.

Instantly overcome by need and weakness, she sank back onto the bed. Maybe it didn't matter if she understood why it worked for him. Maybe the important information was that it *did*.

He nibbled higher, making her squirm when he tickled her tummy.

As he kissed his way north, he also reached for the front of her blouse and went to work on the buttons. Seconds later, he flipped open the front catch on her bra and took her right nipple in his mouth.

Glorious didn't begin to describe the sensations filling her body. While he used mouth, lips and tongue to tease her into a frenzy, his hand matched the movements on her other breast. She gasped and writhed, clung to him, pressed closer and begged for more.

There seemed to be a direct connection between her breasts and that place between her thighs. Her legs fell open. She ached and wanted, even as she held him in place.

It was better than she remembered, which she didn't think was possible.

They were both breathing hard. Nicki felt Zane tremble as he continued to touch her and she didn't think she could hold out much longer.

"Get naked," she whispered.

He didn't need to be told twice. He stood up and grinned, then went to work on his clothes. Seconds later he stood before her, undressed and aroused.

She stared at his broad chest, at the pattern of dark hair that led down to his flat belly and the thick maleness jutting toward her. Had she been standing, she would have gone weak in the knees. As she was lying down, she was able to stay relatively in control.

She shifted back on the bed while he moved next to her. Then their hands were all over each other. While he traced the curve of her hip and the length of her leg, she stroked his back, his rear and the top of his thigh before settling her hand on him.

She rubbed back and forth, then slipped her thumb over the soft, velvety tip. His breath caught in a ragged gasp.

"So you want to play that game," he whispered just before pressing an open kiss on the sensitive skin below her ear. His tongue flicked back and forth, causing goose bumps to break out on her arms.

At the same time he slipped a hand between her

legs and moved his fingers through the swollen dampness. Now it was her turn to gasp, then writhe as he searched for and found that one place of pleasure.

Electricity jolted through her. She couldn't do anything but close her eyes and let him please her. It was too much—it would never be enough. More, she thought desperately, unable to focus enough to speak the words.

Fortunately, Zane was able to read her mind. He shifted his hand so his thumb pressed against her most sensitive spot and his finger dipped inside. Then he moved both, delighting her, making her hips buck, her head fall back and her entire body tense in anticipation.

She was already so close. Too close. She wanted to tell him to wait, to let her savor the moment. She wanted to take her time. But it was too late.

As his thumb circled and his finger mimicked the act of love to follow, he claimed her with a kiss that touched her soul. Mouths pressed, breaths exchanged, she lost herself in the pleasure. Her release swept through her, a violent storm that battered her senses and left her shaking with ecstasy.

Zane continued to touch her, lighter and lighter until he barely brushed against her throbbing flesh. When she was able to finally open her eyes, she found him looking at her. Not smiling, not speaking, just watching.

"Thank you," he murmured at last.

His tender words made her eyes burn, but she blinked away the tears and reached for him. When he was inside, stretching her, filling her, making her reach again for the moment of release, she found that it was her turn to watch him. Even as pleasure claimed her a second time, she saw the tension in his face, the near grimace of his mouth as he pumped in and out, reaching for his own climax.

At that crucial moment, when they were both lost in the wonder of what their bodies could do together, their gazes locked. She saw down to his very essence and knew he had the same view of her.

For a split second, time stood still. Shy, bruised and lonely souls kissed in a moment of connection so profound, she had no words. This wasn't just making love, Nicki thought, this was two becoming one.

They clung to each other until their bodies returned to normal. Then Zane rolled on his side, pulling her with him.

She braced herself for his casual response to what she'd considered a life-altering experience, but he didn't speak. Instead he maneuvered them both under the covers, then pulled her close and stroked her hair.

Nicki knew it was crazy, but she had the overwhelming need to cry. She wasn't sad—if anything she was more content than she'd ever been. But she was also terrified.

Something had happened. Something more scary than when she'd broken her legs and been told she wouldn't ever walk again. Even as she lay there, safe in Zane's embrace, she could feel something shifting inside. It was as if her heart were physically opening up and allowing him to be a part of her.

She hadn't wanted to fall in love with him, but what if it was too late? What if she already had?

If she loved him, she would want him to love her back. If she loved him, then leaving and starting somewhere else wasn't possible. Loving Zane would mean needing him as much as she needed air or food or sleep. He would weave himself into the very fabric of her being and then what? Would he love her back? And if he didn't, how long would it be until he left and she had to learn to survive without him?

I love you.

The words hovered on her lips, but she didn't speak them. Not yet. Maybe not ever.

Loving Zane. Could she be more of a fool? He was a man who never committed. He didn't do long-term or forever. He did temporary and meaningless.

He kissed her forehead. "I want to stay here with you tonight."

She nodded because speaking would mean saying what she was thinking. What she was feeling.

"Are you hungry?" he asked. "We have those dinners."

She shook her head.

He sat up and looked at her. "What's wrong? Are you okay?"

She was far from all right, but she wasn't going to tell him that, either.

"Hold me," she whispered.

"I am."

"More. Hold me more."

He slipped back down onto the mattress and wrapped both arms around her. She turned so she could lean her head against his shoulder and breathe in the scent of him.

"Shh," he murmured. "I'm right here. I'm not going anywhere."

She believed him. For tonight. But what about tomorrow and the rest of her life?

Chapter Nine

Nicki managed to get some sleep that night. By the next morning, she'd convinced herself that worrying about being in love with Zane was a subject best explored in the privacy of her own home…when she was alone. So when she felt him lightly tracing the length of her spine, she was able to turn toward him and smile.

"You snore," he said as he kissed the tip of her nose.

"I do not."

"Okay, you don't, but you breathe deeply when you're asleep. I'll bet you're going to snore when you're an old lady."

"Is this your idea of sweet talk the morning after?"

"Yup." He grinned and got up. "So here's the thing," he said as he stretched. "It's Wednesday."

She admired the view of his very naked self and

leaned back to enjoy the show. "I was aware of that, but thanks for sharing."

"You're welcome." He plopped down on the edge of the bed, on her side. "We're supposed to go back to Seattle this morning."

"I know that as well."

He was so close, she couldn't resist tiptoeing her fingers across his bare leg. As she got closer to the promised land, the body part in question seemed to notice. There was a slight stirring, then it began to grow.

Zane glared at her. "I'm trying to have a serious conversation."

"Oh, and we can't do that if I'm doing this?"

She took him in her hand and moved back and forth along the rapidly hardening length. Then she fluttered her eyelashes at him.

"Not enough oxygen going to your brain?" she asked.

He closed his eyes and gave himself up to the caress for a couple of minutes, then grabbed her wrist. "I thought we'd save that for after breakfast."

"Interesting plan, but we have a plane to catch."

"Which is my point. I have a business trip on Friday. I have to fly to New York to meet with the prince and princess of El Bahar. They're planning an extended trip to the States with their three children and they want to have local security to supplement whatever palace guards they're bringing."

She was having a little trouble tearing her attention away from his arousal. She couldn't help thinking how much more pleasant this conversation would be with him inside of her.

"I fail to see how your business trip has anything

to do with us doing the wild thing again.'' She teased the very tip of him with her finger.

He sucked in a breath. ''My point is I want to call Jeff and tell him we're staying an extra day. The plane isn't needed back. I don't have anything pressing on my calendar, do you?''

One more day with Zane? One more night in this beautiful hotel before heading back to the real world?

''I like a man with a plan,'' she said. ''My calendar is blissfully empty.''

''Great.'' He rose and collected bathrobes from the closet, then tossed her one. ''You call down for room service while I check in with Jeff.''

He shrugged into the robe. After pushing her wheelchair to the edge of the bed and locking it into place, he picked up his jacket and dug around for his cell phone.

Nicki had a sudden thought. ''What are you going to tell him?'' she asked.

''That we want to celebrate the new contract by staying an extra day.''

She felt heat on her cheeks. ''You can't say that. He's going to suspect something.''

''Like what?''

''Like we're doing it.''

Zane grinned. ''I swear that my business partner never wants to think about me doing it. Even if he were to find us naked on your desk, he wouldn't want to think about it. Trust me. It's a guy thing.''

That may be true, Nicki thought as Zane dialed the office, but what about Ashley? She knew what had happened before and if Jeff told her that Nicki and Zane had spent an extra night in L.A. she would be able to put all the pieces together.

''Please don't share the completed puzzle with your husband,'' Nicki whispered as she shifted into the chair, then wheeled to the desk for the room service menu.

As they'd both skipped dinner, they were starving by the time the breakfast cart was wheeled into their room. Zane signed for the charge while Nicki poured coffee and pulled lids off of dishes. There was very little conversation for the first few minutes, until they took the edge off their hunger.

Nicki took in the view, which included Zane and the open French doors behind him. It was a clear morning, with a brilliant blue sky.

''So Jeff didn't want to know why we were staying?'' she asked.

''He said we'd done great and to have a good time.''

She wasn't sure she liked that. ''What was his tone of voice? Was he joking?''

Zane pushed back his plate and reached for his coffee. ''I have no idea about his tone. He was fine, we're staying an extra day, so let it go.''

Easier said than done. She didn't usually skip workdays, which meant she had tons of vacation time built up. But as they were already here, she might as well enjoy herself.

''Come out onto the balcony,'' he said. ''We can sit in the sunshine for a few minutes.''

He led the way, then settled on a big cushion he'd brought out and leaned his shoulder against her legs. She held her coffee in one hand and stroked his hair with the other.

She wasn't any less terrified than she'd been the

night before, but she was learning to cope with the feeling of impending panic. When they returned to Seattle and she had a few days to herself, she would work out a plan. In the meantime, she would simply enjoy their time together.

Something soft brushed against her knee. She glanced down and saw Zane tracing the line of the scars on her leg.

"Do they ever hurt?" he asked.

"Not the scars. There are some achy places inside. If I exercise too hard, or use my braces for too long I can feel it."

He turned and grinned at her. "These aren't all that impressive."

"Oh, you think not?"

He shrugged out of his robe and exposed his back to her. "Now that's a scar," he said.

She studied the long narrow line slicing by his shoulder blade. "A knife?"

"Wicked, huh?"

"Very nice." There was another scar by his rib cage. "Gun shot?"

"Uh-huh."

"Did you get these while you were in the Marines or are they from your previous life?"

He pulled the robe back over his shoulders and turned to face her. "I got them in the service."

He didn't talk about his past much, which made her wonder why. "Can you tell me what you did?"

His eyes clouded. "I was a sniper."

Four simple words, yet they stunned her into silence. A sniper? She had a feeling that was a polite way of saying he'd killed people. But who and where? And who had shot back?

So many questions. Rather than ask them and spoil the day, she shifted to another topic.

"So you went into the military to get yourself straightened out, right? I remember you saying you got in trouble for stealing a truck."

"Not just a truck," he corrected with a grin. "A truck filled with stolen televisions."

"Not exactly a smart thing to do."

"It was only dumb when I got caught. As it was my first offense, the judge sent me to one of those boot-camp reform schools instead of prison. I found I liked the discipline of the service and enlisted when I turned eighteen."

She thought of her own happy childhood, of the parents who had doted on her. "Where was your family?"

He shrugged. "Gone. I never knew my dad. My mom took off when I was three or four, so my grandmother raised me. She wanted more for me than life in the streets or dying young in a gang. I didn't know any other world. So in some ways, getting caught was the best thing that ever happened to me."

"You've come a long way."

"Up and out."

"Why did you leave the Marines?"

The shadows returned to his eyes, and with them came a stiffness to his body. She could feel the ghosts circling them and wondered if they belonged to the living or the dead.

"You don't have to tell me," she said.

He shrugged. "I got hurt pretty bad. I knew that if I kept doing what I was doing I'd end up dead. One day I didn't want that, so I left. I met up with Jeff about two weeks later and we started the company."

She wanted to know where he'd been when he'd been hurt and why he'd thought dying was better than living. She wanted to know what had changed his mind.

Before she could decide on what questions to ask, Zane took her coffee cup from her hand and set it on a small glass table, then swept her into his arms. She shrieked.

"Where are we going?" she asked.

He nuzzled her neck. "To take a shower. I noticed there's a very interesting bench in the master bath and it's at just the right height."

She looped her arm around his neck and smiled. "The right height for what?"

"I'll show you."

Zane deposited Nicki on the counter, then dropped his robe to the floor and walked into the spacious shower to start the water. When it was the right temperature, he turned back to collect her, then had to stop dead when he saw that she, too, had shrugged out of her robe.

The white terry cloth pooled at her waist, exposing her breasts to view. She might not be as well endowed as most of the women he'd taken to bed, but she was still perfect. Her sweet curves begged to be touched, explored and tasted while the peach-colored nipples pointed right at him in a saucy "come and get it" kind of way.

In the three steps it took to cross to her, he was already hard. It took every ounce of self control to keep from burying himself into her waiting warmth. But he had plans for their shower, so instead of giving in to what he guessed they both wanted, he carried her into the steamy shower and set her on the bench.

"What do you think?" he asked as he knelt in front of her and let the water dance over both of them.

She smiled. "This could be interesting."

"More than that," he promised.

Humor brightened her eyes, and passion. She wanted, just like he did. For a second, the past threatened. He knew better than to talk about it, but being around her had somehow lulled him into lowering his guard. It wouldn't happen again, he told himself. It couldn't.

He brushed those thoughts away and reached for the soap. After lathering it between his hands, he touched her everywhere, as much to excite as to cleanse.

He stroked the length of her arms and her back, then cupped her breasts. He slid his hands down her belly, along her legs, then returned to slip them between her thighs. When her breathing was ragged and he could feel her pulsing toward him, he shifted out of the way so the spray could rinse her. Then he lowered his head and tasted her.

The intimate kiss made her gasp. She clung to him, digging her hands into his shoulders. Her legs parted more as she moaned. Water washed them both, while steam surrounded them.

He tasted her, drank of her and the water. When he inserted a single finger into her waiting slickness, she arched back and convulsed around him. He felt the spasms of her orgasm as he continued to flick his tongue against that single point of pleasure. He drew out the contact until she sighed her completion. Only then did he straighten and smile at her.

Her eyes opened slowly. She looked deeply relaxed and satisfied.

"Talk about a great way to start my day," she said. "Wow."

He grinned and reached for the soap.

"I'll do that," she said and proceeded to wash him down.

She had him stand and turn away so she could do his back and the backs of his legs. When he faced her again, she had a gleam in her eye that told him there was about to be the best kind of trouble.

"Ready?" she asked as she lathered her hands again.

He already knew, but he couldn't help asking, "For what?"

She dropped the soap and put her hands on his hardness. The slick pressure was erotic and mind bending. He felt his knees give way and he had to lock them in place.

Back and forth, back and forth. Pressure built at the base of his arousal. He'd planned on sitting down and having her straddle him but right now he couldn't imagine moving.

When she pushed him back into the spray, he didn't understand, but when she pulled him close and leaned forward, everything clicked into place.

As her mouth settled over him, he braced himself against the shower walls. The water pummeled his back while her lips and tongue worked magic between his legs.

Need built. He swore. He groaned her name. Then he lost control in the best way possible.

"You can't be serious," Nicki said late that morning as she wheeled across the parking lot.

"Why not? We want to hang out and have fun,"

Zane told her. "What better place?" He tugged on a strand of her hair. "The park is completely wheel-chair accessible. I spoke to the concierge at the hotel and she assured me they have a sterling reputation for that sort of thing."

"I know, but Disneyland?"

Nicki stared at the castle rising against the blue sky and the white mountain where three climbers made their way to the top. She could hear the excited conversation all around her.

Zane looked at her. "Don't you want to go?"

She bit her lower lip, not sure how to explain that she'd only been once—the year before her accident—and that she'd always wanted to go back. But somehow she'd never made the time and now they were here and the fact that Zane had been the one to think of it made her want to burst into tears. Or do it with him right there by the entrance.

"I'm delighted," she said when she was sure she could speak without her voice cracking.

"Good."

They had a heated discussion about which ride to go on first, then agreed to alternating picks with a coin toss to determine who went first. The resulting schedule meant dashing from one side of the park to the other—perhaps not the most sensible plan, but one that was lots of fun.

"Hurry," Nicki called as she maneuvered through the crowd on her way to the Haunted House. "Jeez, Zane, you're such a slowpoke."

He caught up with her by the entrance. "You're too fast on those damn wheels."

"Zane was beaten by a girl," she said in a singsong voice.

He bent low and kissed her. "Sugar, you can beat me any time you want...just so long as you're wearing black leather."

Black leather? Her eyes widened and she had a feeling she looked stunned. But before she could pursue that line of conversation, they were moving toward the front of the mansion and surrounded by children.

"I'll be bringing that up later," she told him.

"I'm counting on it."

The helpful staff took possession of her wheelchair while she sat through the charming ride. At the end, when a ghost "tried to follow them home" Zane put his arm around her and told the green visitor that, "No one is going to get my girl."

Nicki tried not to read too much into the words. She and Zane were hanging out together, and she knew that he liked her, but that was a long way from what *she* was experiencing. Still, his possessiveness made her feel all warm inside.

They headed toward Main Street. They still had about a half hour before heading for the Blue Bayou Restaurant and their dinner reservations.

"Let's go in here," he said, pointing her toward one of the big shops that lined the street.

Once inside, Nicki found herself wanting to buy one of everything. There were stuffed animals, watches, T-shirts, collectible cartoon cells.

Zane made her laugh when he tried on mouse ears, then picked up three glowing rubber balls and started to juggle. Talk about another surprise—he wasn't half-bad.

"Betcha Brad can't do this," he said as he caught the third ball and dropped them back into the counter.

"You're right."

There were a lot of things Boyd hadn't been able to do. The biggest had been to help her get over Zane. Now it was too late. Watching him move through the store, joking with the sales staff, offering to buy her everything from a stuffed Simba to mouse ears of her own, she felt her heart tighten with love. Zane was everything she'd ever wanted. And for this moment in time, he was hers.

She studied a collection of postcards, then decided to pick several to help her remember the day. A burst of laughter caught her attention. Turning, she saw three young women hovering around Zane. They stared at him with obvious interest.

Nicki allowed herself a moment of envy for their easy walks and long, healthy legs. Then she shook off the feeling and reminded herself that her life was exactly what she wanted it to be.

A minute or so later Zane walked away from the women. His gaze settled on her and when he smiled she knew he was thinking about last night and this morning. Those young women had never even registered.

Happiness bubbled inside of her. When Zane approached, she grabbed his shirtfront and pulled him down so she could kiss him…thoroughly.

When she released him, he crouched next to her and smiled. "What was that for?"

"No particular reason. I just wanted to connect."

"Good."

He pulled something out of his shirt pocket. A small box. When he opened it she saw he'd bought her a gold charm bracelet decorated with a pair of mouse ears.

"So you can remember our day together," he said as he fastened the catch.

As if she could ever forget. "Thank you, Zane."

He touched his index finger to the tip of her nose. "You're welcome."

The plane landed shortly after eleven the next morning. Zane carried Nicki down the steps and set her into her wheelchair while the copilot collected their luggage from the hold.

"You said you're taking the rest of the day off," Zane said as he followed her to her van. "You need to get some rest."

She smiled at the worried tone of his voice. "You slept as little as I did." They'd both been up most of last night, making love.

He shrugged. "I'll catch up tonight and on the plane tomorrow."

That's right. His New York trip. She would miss him, but wasn't sure if she should tell him.

She clicked the remote unlock button. "I promise to get plenty of rest, both today and tonight."

"I'll call you from the hotel," he promised. "You know. Just to check in."

She liked that he wanted to check in, even as she told herself it didn't mean anything. Zane was being nice, nothing more. As for what was going on between them...she'd already decided that would stay undefined until he got back from his trip. Then she would have a talk with him. Well, assuming she had the courage. There were times when she thought it was better not to know what he was thinking about them.

The copilot set her luggage on the ramp and she

thanked him. Then she wheeled onto the ramp and pushed the button to raise it.

When she was level with the rear of the van, she looked at Zane. "Have a good trip."

He moved close and kissed her. "I'll miss you."

His words made her chest tightened. "Me, too."

He tucked her hair behind her ears. "What happens if Boyd calls while I'm gone?"

"Jealous?" She chuckled. "Not to worry. I told you, we broke up."

"Just see that it stays that way."

A delicious thrill shot through her. Maybe this time was different. Maybe Zane was interested in more than temporary and short-term.

He gave her another quick kiss. "Drive safe," he said.

She nodded and headed for the front of the van.

Less than forty minutes later, she was in her house with her suitcase open on her bed. As she unpacked, she found herself humming softly and smiling for no reason at all.

Okay, she had it bad. Worse than bad. She was a woman in love and was there anything sappier than that?

As Nicki picked up the shirt she'd worn to Disneyland, she recalled their romantic dinner with a view of the water. Okay, most of the plants had been plastic and there had been noisy kids all around them, but the room had also sparkled from the white lights and Zane had stared at her as if she were the most precious woman on the planet. He'd made her feel special and whole and normal.

She collected another blouse and dropped them into her laundry basket. She supposed that was Zane's greatest gift—his ability to see her as just like everyone else.

She'd been nervous about sharing a room with him, but he'd made everything so easy. She'd never remembered to be embarrassed. If a moment had threatened to turn awkward, he'd distracted her with a joke or a kiss, or both. While she'd had lovers before, she'd never been that *intimate* with a man.

Nicki picked up her makeup case and carried it into the specially modified bathroom. There wasn't a tub. Instead an oversized shower stood in the corner. It was specially designed so that she could wheel right in. There was a wide bench, grip bars and a nonskid floor. In the past she'd always hated her shower, seeing it as a symbol of what she couldn't do. Now remembering making love in the hotel shower, she saw the shower as filled with possibilities. Most of them sexual.

It didn't matter if she never had sex in her modified bathroom; she knew she could. Another gift Zane had given her.

As she unpacked her makeup, she watched the movement of the mouse ears on her bracelet. Light bounced off the curved gold and danced on the walls. Smiling, she bent down to set her cosmetics on their shelf. Her gaze landed on the pink box of supplies for her period.

It was one of those odd moment in space and time when the world seemed to stop turning. She moved, she breathed and yet nothing was as it should be. As if from a great distance, she reached out to touch the box. Her fingers barely grazed the front, then her hand fell to her side. Bone-cold panic seeped into her midsection.

In that heartbeat, Nicki knew.

She told herself it wasn't possible, even though it was. She told herself no one was that stupid, even though she had been.

That first night she and Zane had made love on her sofa, then later in her bed. How many times? Two? Three? They'd made love without protection and she'd never once considered the potential disaster.

Why? Where was her brain? She was always careful. Usually she was on the Pill. Just not in the past few months.

There'd been that night, then the past couple of days. Not once had birth control crossed her mind. How could she have been so irresponsible? Or dumb?

Closing her eyes, she did some quick calculations. She was late. More than a little late. She was late by at least ten days.

After dumping the rest of her makeup into the sink, she turned and raced to the front of the house. She collected her purse and her keys, then made her way to the van.

It took thirty-seven minutes to drive to the drugstore, make her purchase, return home and pee on a stick. Thirty-seven minutes after which her life changed forever.

She was pregnant.

Chapter Ten

Nicki didn't sleep that night, and she hadn't slept the previous two nights in Los Angeles, so she was pretty much a basket case by the time she pulled into work the following morning. She considered calling in sick, but she knew Zane would get word of that and demand to know what was wrong. As she hadn't quite figured that out herself, she didn't know how she was going to have the conversation with him. No, better to muddle through the day and head home early.

Complicating matters was a headache she knew was only going to get worse. If she was pregnant there were no more cups of coffee in her immediate future, which meant she was going to suffer with caffeine withdrawal. After all she had to do what was right for the baby.

Baby! She still couldn't believe it. Of course she

only had herself to blame. Previously she'd been on the Pill whenever she'd been sexually involved with a man, and she'd always insisted he use protection. With Zane... She locked her van and headed for the building. She'd just plain forgotten to take care of things.

She knew he wasn't like most people who assumed that because she was in a wheelchair she couldn't get pregnant. How many times had she had to explain that nonworking legs didn't mean nonworking ovaries. Zane knew she was on the Pill. He teased her about it. So it would never have occurred to him that she wasn't safe.

"Complications to mull over another time," she told herself as she entered the building. Now that she was here, she would do her best to focus on her job and push the rest of it out of her mind. There was nothing she had to do about the baby today, and with Zane gone, no one she had to tell.

She made her way into her office where she found stacks of paperwork and phone messages waiting for her. She'd barely finished organizing her in-basket when Jeff stopped by to see her.

"Great work," he said, taking the chair across from hers. "Mr. Sabotini couldn't say enough good things about you."

She smiled. "He was very charming, and very worried about his children."

"We already have the team in place." Jeff tossed another file on her desk. "This job is going to bring us a lot more work. The company will grow and you'll be a part of that."

Nicki knew that Jeff and Zane rewarded employees who worked well and she didn't doubt she would find something extra in her next paycheck. For a second she thought about asking for extended maternity leave instead, but reconsidered. Jeff might not know that she and Zane were more than friends, but he wasn't an idiot. He would put things together fairly quickly and then who knew what would happen. Better for her to be the one to tell Zane he was going to be a father.

She must have paled at the thought because Jeff leaned toward her and frowned.

"You okay?"

No. Not even close. She sighed. "I'm fine. Just the rigors of travel catching up with me."

Jeff grinned. "Zane said you went to Disneyland yesterday. How rigorous could it have been?"

She chuckled. "Hey, there was a lot of walking."

"Very funny." He rose. "Why don't you head out early today. Consider it part of your reward for a job well done."

"That would be great. Thanks."

She waited until Jeff left, then picked up the phone. There was only one person she could think of who could possibly understand what she was going through.

She waited until Ashley was on the phone. "It's me," she said. "If I leave work early this afternoon, would you have time to talk?"

Zane had dealt with a lot of rich people over the past few years. In his business, they were usually his clients. But the prince and princess of El Bahar were his first shot at royalty. He was pleasantly surprised by how the meeting was going.

"El Bahar is neutral," he said to the royals, "but terrorists don't care about things like that."

Prince Jamal nodded. "I agree. Heidi and I are concerned about striking a balance between relative normalcy and overprotection. We also have the children to consider."

Princess Heidi, an American who had married into the ruling family of El Bahar, smiled at him. "Jamal and I thought people more familiar with the lay of the land, so to speak, would be assets to our existing security team."

"We often have to work with a team in place," Zane told her. "Our personnel don't have a problem with that."

"Good."

Despite the designer clothing and impressive jewels, Princess Heidi seemed like a down-to-earth person. When her husband left to make a call, she smiled at him.

"I understand you're from Seattle," she said. "It's a very beautiful part of the country."

He nodded. "A lot of green. Nothing like El Bahar."

"True. We're a desert nation, but when we get the rains, a surprising number of plants seem to spring to life overnight."

He'd never spoken with royalty before, so he wasn't sure what was allowed. Still, he knew Nicki would be interested in his encounter with a real live princess, so he decided to risk the potential protocol breach.

"You're American."

The princess grinned. "Technically I'm a citizen of El Bahar. Marrying one of the princes makes that a requirement. But in my heart, I belong to both countries. That's one of the reasons I want us to spend more time here. So our children can see what life is like in the West." Her smile faded. "While the people of El Bahar have always welcomed those from other countries, there are extremists in nearby nations who don't share those liberal beliefs."

"Both El Bahar and Bahania are excellent examples of the peace that is possible in the Middle East," he said.

"True and a good thing, what with all three of the El Baharain princes marrying Americans." Her smile returned. "It was something of a scandal."

He chuckled. "And now the same thing is happening in Bahania. I understand that one of the king's sons married an American."

"You're right," Heidi told him. "In fact Princess Cleo is from your own Washington state."

Prince Jamal returned to the hotel conference room and sat down. "Where were we?" he asked.

When the meeting concluded, Zane collected his papers and an extra copy of the proposal. After closing his briefcase, he pulled out his cell phone and dialed the office. He was put through to Jeff.

"I want a big raise," he said by way of greeting.

"And here I thought it was my job to bring in new clients while you were busy risking your life on the job."

"Send me back out in the field," Zane said easily.

"Maybe not. I already have an official fax from the El Baharain office of royal security. We've been retained."

Zane detailed the high points, then waited while Jeff put him through to Nicki.

"You should have been here," he told her.

"Really?"

"Sure. I just sat across from a genuine princess. Pretty cool, huh?"

He heard the smile in Nicki's voice as she said, "So you head off for the east coast and less than twenty four hours later, you're infatuated by a princess? What kind of loyalty is that?"

He grinned. "Don't sweat it. Even if I didn't think you were hot enough to be irresistible, she's married. And her husband looked like the kind of guy who would throw anyone messing with his wife into shackles for a couple hundred years."

"Was she nice?"

"Very."

"Attractive?"

"Sure, but not my type." Especially not when he couldn't get a certain redhead out of his mind. "Want me to see if I can steal a couple of pieces of her jewelry?"

"I doubt it's my style. I'm a simple girl at heart."

"Simple tastes or simple-minded?"

She laughed. "Very funny." The humor faded. "When are you coming home?"

"In a couple of days. I have meetings with their security people tomorrow and Monday morning. I have a flight out early in the afternoon."

"Okay."

He straightened. There was something about how she said the word. Something that made him wonder if everything was all right.

"What's going on?" he asked.

"Nothing."

"You okay?"

"I'm fine. I swear." She cleared her throat. "Why don't you come to dinner Monday night? You can tell me all about the princess."

"Sure. I'd like that."

There was a brief pause. For a second Zane thought about telling Nicki that he missed her, but he stopped himself before he said the words.

Wanting, he reminded himself. Not missing. Missing wasn't allowed. He'd made it a point to never get involved with someone he *could* miss. Had Nicki changed that? He'd always cared about her, but things were different now. Confusing.

Still he knew the danger of getting too involved. No way that was going to happen.

"You going to be around on Sunday?" he asked.

"I think so. Why?"

"I thought I might give you a call."

"That would be nice."

"Great. I'll talk to you then and I'll see you on Monday. I'll bring wine."

Nicki hesitated, then said that would be fine.

When he hung up, he heard a sound and turned. Princess Heidi stood in the doorway of the conference room. She smiled sheepishly.

"Okay," she told him. "I was shamelessly eavesdropping. I can't help it. I'm a sucker for couples in love."

"No problem," Zane said with a casualness he didn't feel. In love? Not even on a bet. He didn't do love. Not ever. He knew the price of loving…and losing, and he'd vowed to never pay it again.

Ashley walked back into the living room and collapsed on the sofa. "I'm sure he's finally asleep," she said and sighed. "He's only eighteen months old. The terrible twos aren't supposed to start for another six months, but he's already making trouble." She checked her watch. "Maggie won't be back from her play date for another hour and half, so we're on our own."

"Great."

Nicki fingered the hem of her sweater, then shifted in her chair. She'd been the one to request the meeting with her friend, so it was up to her to get things started. It's not as if Ashley knew what was wrong.

But she didn't know what to say, which led to an interesting dilemma. If she couldn't say the words to her best friend, how on earth was she going to tell Zane?

A bridge to cross when she next saw him.

"I'm—" She closed her eyes, then opened them.

Ashley tilted her head. Concern darkened her eyes. "Are you sick or dying?"

"No, I'm perfectly healthy." Pregnancy was a condition, not a disease, right?

"Good." Ashley smiled. "I was a little worried. You sounded so serious on the phone and you haven't been yourself since you arrived. What's going on? Is it Zane? Jeff told me you two spent an extra day in L.A. I thought that might mean things had started up again."

"They did, but that's not really the problem." She reconsidered the statement. "Okay, it's part of the problem, but not the big part."

"That's clear." Ashley leaned toward her. "Just start at the beginning or blurt it out. I can't think of a single thing you could tell me that would be the least bit shocking."

Nicki swallowed. "I'm pregnant."

Ashley blinked. "Okay. Except for that. Pregnant? Are you sure?"

"I used four different home pregnancy tests. They were all positive."

"Okay then. You probably are. Wow." Ashley grinned. "Are you happy? I know it's unexpected, but still, a baby. That's so wonderful."

Nicki opened her mouth to protest, then closed it. Ashley was right. A baby *was* wonderful. And amazing. Funny how she'd been so busy mentally ranting about how stupid she'd been to not use birth control that she'd never stopped to consider that there was a precious life growing inside of her. She'd always wanted kids. Maybe not this way, but that was okay.

She smiled. "It is great, isn't it?"

"I'm guessing Zane's the father."

"He's the only one I've been sleeping with."

Ashley shook her head. "I take it he doesn't know."

"Not yet. He's in New York and I didn't want to tell him over the phone. He's coming to dinner Monday night. I'll spring it on him then."

"Any idea what he's going to say?"

Nicki had been doing her best not to think about that. "Not really." She wasn't sure she wanted to know.

Ashley rose and hugged her. "I think this is fabulous. You'll be a great mom."

Nicki hugged her back. "I hope so. I never thought about doing it on my own. How did you manage all those years with Maggie?"

Ashley resumed her seat. "It was a struggle," she admitted. "I didn't have your education or health insurance. Honestly, there were times I could barely keep food on the table. I was working nights, going to school during the day. The only thing that kept me going was how much I loved Maggie and that light at the end of the tunnel. I knew when I finally finished my degree, life would get easier for both of us.''

"Then you met Jeff and he swept you off your feet.''

Ashley's expression softened. "Something like that. He was scary at first. A little distant. Maggie won him over right away. I think watching him fall for her made me start to fall myself.'' She raised her eyebrows. "But there is definitely something in the water at that company.''

"What do you mean?''

"I was pregnant before Jeff and I married. In fact he'd told me he couldn't have children.'' She waved her hand. "It's a complicated story. Anyway, there I was pregnant. And here you are. You're definitely keeping the baby, right?''

Nicki nodded slowly. "Now that you mention it, I never considered any other option.'' She couldn't give up her child. "I'll spend all my time terrified, but I can raise a baby on my own. I have resources.''

"Me, for one.''

Nicki glanced at Ashley's stomach. "Right, because with two kids and a third on the way, you'll have so much free time.''

"I can at least give you advice.''

"I'll need plenty of that. I have money. Not just my salary, but money from the settlement.''

"What settlement?''

"When I broke my legs.'' She explained about the accident at the resort. "I don't know if my parents would have sued them or not. Before any decision was made, the owners offered a large settlement. My folks accepted on my behalf.''

Ashley grinned. "So you're secretly rich?"

"I have a nest egg. My parents' insurance covered most of my medical expenses so very little of the settlement got used for that. They invested the money and it did well. I spent some of it remodeling my house but the rest just sits there. Between my salary and my savings, I shouldn't have to touch it, but it's nice to know it's there.''

"More than nice,'' Ashley told her. "It's one less thing to worry about. Are your parents going to freak out?''

Nicki considered the question. "I don't know. They always wanted me to get married and have a family. I think they'll be happy about the baby, even if they're worried about me.'' She smiled sheepishly. "I checked our insurance coverage. I'm entitled to eight weeks maternity leave with pay and six weeks without for maternity leave. I was thinking I could even work from home.''

"If Jeff doesn't agree to that, you let me know.''

Nicki laughed. "Because you'll take him on?''

"You bet.'' Ashley leaned forward. "You'll need to start looking for day care. What about having someone come in and stay with you?''

"I would like that. I'm sure my folks will come up for the first few weeks, while I'm still in the panic stage.''

"You know, we've talked about everything but the baby's father,'' her friend said. "Are you scared about telling him?''

"Wouldn't you be?''

"Sure."

Nicki touched her stomach. "I don't know what to say. I guess there isn't a good way to break it gently. At the same time I want him to understand that I'm perfectly capable of raising this child on my own."

"Is that what you want?"

"It's what makes the most sense. Zane isn't going to be interested in having a family. He's just not that kind of man."

"He could surprise you."

Nicki knew it was too dangerous to have those kind of hopes. But in her heart, that was what she wanted. For him to be thrilled by the news and instantly confess his undying love for her. Then they could get married and live happily ever after. The thing was, she had a feeling life wasn't going to be that tidy.

"Zane doesn't do permanent commitments," she said. "He's not going to want to be a father. I doubt he'll want to be involved at all."

Ashley shook her head. "I think you're wrong and that he'll surprise you, but we'll have to wait and see. You said he's coming over Monday night?"

"Right. For dinner."

"I have a word of advice."

"What?"

Ashley smiled. "Before you tell him, get him a drink. A really big one. He's going to need it."

Chapter Eleven

Zane arrived at Nicki's house about fifteen minutes early. He'd brought roses and a bottle of wine. The flowers weren't his style, but when he'd driven by a florist on the way over, he'd found himself pulling into the parking lot. Once inside the store, he'd seen peach-colored roses that he'd had to buy. Which made him feel like some high-school kid taking out the prom queen.

But anticipation was stronger than his chagrin. Maybe he shouldn't have missed Nicki, but he'd spent the past four days counting the hours until he saw her again. She'd invited him for dinner and he was hoping she planned to keep him around until breakfast.

When he knocked on the front door, she called that it was open. He stepped inside.

"What if I'd been a serial killer?" he asked as he closed the door behind himself.

Nicki sat in her chair in the entrance to the living room. She smiled. "Then you wouldn't have knocked."

He crossed toward her. "You work for a security company. You know better."

"You're right."

He grinned. "My favorite two words in the world." He set the wine on the floor, the flowers on her lap, then bent down and cupped her face. "Hi."

"Hi, yourself."

Makeup accentuated the wide shape of her beautiful green eyes. Her mouth was full and inviting. She smelled exotic and sexy. Her casual dress fell to the knee and left the rest of her legs bare. He noticed she wasn't wearing stockings, which was probably for the best. Knowing about her garter belt would have made it impossible for him to concentrate.

He pressed his mouth to hers, meaning the contact to be a friendly greeting. But the second their lips touched, his blood heated and he wanted more. He leaned in a little. Nicki touched his cheek, then shifted her head slightly.

"The flowers are beautiful," she said. "Thank you."

Zane straightened. "You're welcome."

Was it his imagination or had she just pulled away from him? He studied her, searching for clues. He couldn't find even one. Her smile seemed genuine, her gaze was steady.

"I need to get them in water," she said as she turned and wheeled toward the back of the house.

Zane picked up the wine and trailed after her. "What's for dinner?"

"Lasagna. My mother's recipe."

"I'm impressed."

"You should be. I had to dirty nearly every pan I own to make it. The good news is it freezes well, so I'll have many meals from it."

She stopped in the center of the kitchen and pointed to one of the few tall cabinets. "Vases are in there."

"I remember." He pulled out a glass one and filled it with water. Nicki unwrapped the cellophane and placed the stems into the vase.

"Should I put them on the table?" he asked.

"Sure."

The dining room had already been set for two. He liked how the place settings were so close together. Obviously she had an intimate meal planned. He must have been imagining things with the kiss.

He took a step toward the living room, then pàused. Unless Nicki had regrets about what had happened in L.A. The first time they'd made love, she'd asked that things return to a "friends only" footing. While he hadn't been excited by the idea, he'd agreed because he hadn't wanted to push her. But things were different now. Somehow he was going to have to convince her of that.

He walked into the living room and found her by the sofa. He took a seat close to her.

"How was your flight?"

"What's going on at work?"

They spoke at the same time. Nicki smiled. "You first."

"How's work?" he asked.

"Good. Everyone is very excited about the contract

with the prince and princess. Jeff said Ashley is already talking about vacationing there.''

''With three kids?''

''I don't think it's a thought out plan at this point.''

''They're nice people.''

She raised her eyebrows. ''The prince and princess?''

''Yeah. She's American. Sensible.''

Nicki laughed. ''You mean exotically beautiful.''

''That, too, but I barely noticed.'' He shifted closer, suddenly wanting to tell her that while it probably wasn't a good idea, he *had* missed her. ''Nicki, I—''

She cut him off. ''I haven't offered you anything to drink. What would you like? That wine you brought? Does it need to breathe?''

There was something about the way she spoke. Something about her body, as if she were stiff all over. Zane hadn't wanted to see the signs, but as he looked more closely, he saw tension in the set of her mouth and worry in her eyes.

Damn. He knew exactly what was wrong. Okay, maybe he didn't want to hear it, but if Nicki wanted to end their physical relationship, he had no right to stop her. Ignoring the knot in his gut, he took her hands in his.

''I don't need a drink,'' he said, ''but I do need you to tell me what the hell is going on.''

She stared at him. ''I have no idea what you're talking about.''

''Something's wrong. I can sense it.''

She glanced down at their clasped hands, then back at him. ''You're right,'' she said in a low voice.

The knot turned into a vice. Zane wanted to bolt

out of the room. He wanted to demand that she not try to change things. Instead he sat and waited.

"We used to be friends," she said slowly. "Just friends. I liked that. It was certainly much less complicated. Then we went to that party together and you came back here and, well, you know what happened."

"We made love."

She nodded and pulled her hands free. He tried not to take the withdrawal personally. Not that he did a very good job of convincing himself.

"We didn't plan it," she said. "I know it just happened. I don't regret that. I can't. But it changed things."

He braced himself for her rejection. "Then we got back together in Los Angeles."

She frowned. "Yes, but that doesn't really have anything to do with this."

"What? Of course it does. You want us to go back to being friends."

Her eyes widened. "Is that what you think? No, Zane. It's not that at all." She swallowed. "What I'm trying to tell you is that I'm pregnant."

Nicki kept talking, but Zane couldn't hear anything else. He couldn't think, couldn't move. There was only that single word reverberating in his brain.

Pregnant.

Involuntarily his gaze dropped to her stomach. It was as flat as it had ever been. But if she was talking about that first night together, she was only a few weeks along.

He swore silently. The room shifted and instead of Nicki, he saw Amber. Laughing, beautiful Amber telling him that she had a surprise. Amber handing him a small box tied with a yellow ribbon. He'd opened it to find baby booties inside.

He remembered feeling elated beyond words. She was going to have a baby. They were going to be a family. Then he remembered nothing but the fiery explosion that had destroyed his world.

No, he thought as he pushed to his feet. Not again. He couldn't survive it.

"What the hell happened?" he growled.

Nicki's half smile faded. "The usual. You were here that night. We did it more than once and we didn't use protection."

A condom. Right. He *always* used a condom. But he hadn't expected to make love with Nicki so he hadn't had one with him. Not at her place and not in L.A. For the first time in his life, birth control and protection had never crossed his mind.

"You're on the Pill."

"I was," she said apologetically. "I went off a few months ago when I was between guys. I wanted to give my body a rest. Boyd and I didn't seem to be heading into bed, so I didn't think about it." She squared her shoulders. "I didn't do this on purpose."

He knew that, he thought as he paced the length of her living room. Nicki wasn't deceitful. He believed it was just one of those things. It had happened and now they had to deal with it.

His brain flashed again on those tiny baby booties, on Amber's smile, on the heat of the explosion.

No! He couldn't do this. Not again. Not ever. What if Nicki died?

Panic swirled into fear. A fear that crawled inside so deep, he knew he would never get it out.

He looked at her, then headed for the door.

* * *

The slam of the front door echoed in the quiet house. Nicki had expected a lot of reactions, but she'd never thought Zane would bolt. She hurt as if she'd been dragged for miles. But more damaging to the pain in her body was the ache in her soul.

The timer dinged, telling her the lasagna was ready. She knew she had to go take it out of the oven. If she didn't it would burn and what would that accomplish?

She'd thought things would go better. Maybe Zane would be upset or shocked or even mad. Maybe he would yell at her. She'd braced herself for his anger, but she'd never thought he wouldn't react at all. If she lived to be a hundred, she would never forget the blankness that had overtaken his expression. She'd had no way to know what he was thinking, even though she guessed it was bad.

She had been willing to fight with him, to reason, but how was she supposed to battle an empty room?

Forcing herself to move, she headed for the kitchen. After removing the lasagna from the oven and setting it on a hot pad, she leaned back in her chair and fought a wave of nausea.

She had a feeling this upset had nothing to do with the baby and everything to do with her broken heart. Zane hadn't been delighted or confessed his undying love or wanted them to be a family. Apparently he hadn't wanted anything but to be gone.

Only now did she allow herself to admit that if her most pressing fantasy wasn't to come true, she'd hoped that Zane would at least be happy about the child. That he would want to be a part of its life. That they could be a part-time family if nothing else. Apparently that wasn't going to happen, either.

Nicki covered her face with her hands. She had to accept that she was in this alone. That Zane wasn't interested in the baby. Or her.

Tears burned her eyes. She fought them for a couple of seconds, then let them fall. What did it matter if she cried? There wasn't anyone to see or judge.

She wasn't sure how long she sat there. Eventually the tears ran out and she had to go in search of a tissue or five.

In the bright light of her bathroom, with her nose and eyes red and her face blotchy, she was forced to face the truth.

Zane didn't love her. She'd known he wasn't into commitments or long-term relationships when she'd invited him into her bed. He hadn't changed the rules, she had. So it wasn't his fault that she was now left alone and shattered.

While the truth should have cleansed her, instead it only made her want to weep more. If she'd been unable to get over her simple schoolgirl crush on Zane, how would she ever get over being in love with the father of her child?

Zane didn't remember leaving Nicki's house, or driving, but somehow he ended up by the water. As he stared out over the sound, he saw the first wisps of fog forming and felt the chill in the air. Soon the dampness would seep into him. He welcomed the discomfort. Maybe it would distract him from the images filling his brain.

He saw Amber again—laughing, smiling. In his mind, she moved closer and spoke his name, but when he reached for her, she was gone, her presence no more substantial than the fog.

They'd been happy, he remembered, closing his eyes against the present. The clank of the sailboat riggings and the smell of the sea all faded as he recalled warm, sunny days. Happy and content days. For him, it had been a first. He'd grown up on the street. His gang had been his family, but not Amber. She'd been one of four kids, the only girl, and the only child to follow in the family tradition of a life in the military.

They'd met in officer training school, both young and excited about the possibilities of a career with the Marines.

He remembered her as an erotic combination of tough and feminine. Every guy had wanted her, and for reasons he'd never understood, she'd chosen him.

He remembered Amber telling him that eventually one of them was going to have to learn how to cook. Amber insisting they shower together each morning, even when there wasn't any time and they were always late because showering lead to other things. Amber inviting him to spend Christmas with her family then laughingly complaining that it had sure taken him long enough when he'd finally proposed. Amber saying she was pregnant.

Her smile, he thought grimly. He remembered that the most. That and the explosion.

He'd been there. He'd watched her smile and wave as she'd stepped onto the helicopter. He'd stood on the tarmac as the machine rose up and up, then headed east. Suddenly it had swerved and without warning it had plowed into the side of a mountain.

He opened his eyes, but the explosion didn't fade. He could see it, smell it, hear it.

He'd done it, he reminded himself. He'd killed her

as surely as if he'd flown the helicopter into the mountain himself. And now Nicki was pregnant.

The fear returned and with it a metallic taste, like blood on his tongue. Guilt fed the fear until it was all he could feel.

Not again, he told himself. He couldn't go through that again. He couldn't lose Nicki, too.

But he'd been unable to keep Amber safe. How could he protect Nicki and their baby?

Ironic, he thought. His job was to protect others and yet he'd been unable to save those he cared about most.

He clutched the railing, gripping the cold, damp metal until it bit into his hands. He couldn't change the past, but he could secure the future. Somehow he was going to have to make this turn out right. He would explain—make her see why he had to be in charge. Why he had to know everything. He only knew one way to do that.

He climbed back in his car and started the engine.

When he arrived at Nicki's place, he hurried up the walkway, then pounded on the front door.

"Nicki, it's me," he called. He heard the click of a lock.

He could see that she'd been crying. While she was the kind of person who laughed easily, he'd rarely seen her cry and his chest tightened at the thought of him hurting her. He wondered if it would help to tell her *why*.

Later, he thought. First he had to get her to agree. Once he knew he could keep her safe, he could take the time to explain.

"You didn't have to come back," she said. "You made it clear how you feel about this."

"You couldn't be more wrong."

He stepped into the house, then led the way to the living room. When he perched on the edge of the sofa, she stopped several feet away.

"What?" she asked as she wiped the tears from her face. "What do you want?"

Too many things, he thought. A chance to undo what was done. A chance to change the past. As those were unavailable to him he would focus on keeping the future positive—on keeping her and the baby safe.

He rose and crossed to her, then grabbed the arm of her chair and pulled her nearer to the sofa.

Her gasp of outrage didn't surprise him. It was one thing to help her in and out of the company plane, it was another to use her wheelchair against her by pushing her around.

"I need you close," he told her, before she could say anything.

Her tight expression didn't soften, but at least she didn't yell at him.

He leaned toward her and took one of her hands in his. He half expected her to pull away and when she didn't, he took a moment to study her face. Her eyes, the shape of her mouth and her chin. Who would the baby look like? Would it favor one parent over the other, or would it be a blend of both of them? Boy or girl? Did it matter? He shook his head. All he cared about was keeping it from dying. And her.

"I want us to get married right away," he said, speaking quickly. "This week. Tomorrow. We'll get a license and make it happen. Then you'll have my name and I'll be here for you every single minute. I mean that, Nicki. I'm not going anywhere. I want to keep you and the baby safe."

She didn't speak. Her lips had parted slightly and all the color fled her face, but these weren't the kind of signs that would tell him what she was thinking.

He glanced around at her living room. "I'll move in here. I know the houseboat is too hard for you. Plus it wouldn't be safe to have a kid running around right on the water. Which is fine. There's plenty of room. I can pack up a few things tonight, then move the rest of it over the next few days. The houseboat will sell fast. They're always popular. I'll put the money into a trust for you and the baby." He frowned. "I need to get some life insurance, too. And we can start a college fund. Do you have a doctor? Have you seen one? Are you feeling all right?"

There was too much to take in at once, Nicki thought. Even though she knew she was sitting in her chair, she felt as if the room were spinning.

Zane was saying all the right things, but somehow she couldn't believe them. Two hours ago he'd been so stunned by her announcement that he'd walked out without saying anything. Now he was back, talking about them getting married and moving in together. What had changed his mind?

Maybe she would have been a little more quick to jump at his proposal if he'd looked the least bit happy about it. Instead his expression was grim and determined. As if this was a campaign he had to win, regardless of the odds stacked against him. Obviously he wasn't happy about the baby. So why would he sacrifice himself if he—

Then she got it. And with that truth came a pain so sharp, she thought it might slice her in two. She pulled her hand free of his grasp and folded her arms in front of her midsection, as if by pressing hard, she could hold herself together.

Why Zane? She might have expected it from someone else, but never from him. He'd always acted as if the chair didn't matter. Had it just been an act?

Tears threatened, but she willed them away. She would not cry over this. Maybe over the baby and Zane not loving her, but not over this.

"Stop," she said quietly. "Just stop."

He stared at her. "My plan makes sense."

"Not to me." She sighed. "I expected so much more of you, Zane. I thought we were friends."

He stared at her. "What the hell does that have to do with anything?"

"Being in a wheelchair doesn't make me any less capable. I'm perfectly healthy. I will carry this baby to term without any help from you. Being in a wheelchair doesn't mean I can't be a good mother."

He sprang to his feet. "Is that what you think? That this is about you being in a wheelchair? It's not."

He paced the length of her living room, then turned and glared at her. "I don't give a damn about the chair. This is about you and the baby and me wanting to be a part of things. This is about protecting you."

He sounded sincere, but he wasn't making any sense. "Protecting us from what?"

"Everything."

She could see the tension in his body. Obviously he wasn't kidding about all of this, but she didn't know what he was talking about. There was no "everything" to keep her or the baby safe from. Which meant his worries were about her abilities. There was no other reason for him to want to move in and take care of her.

Ever since she'd met Zane, she'd thought he was one of the good guys. That he saw her as a regular person who happened to use a wheelchair to get around. But it wasn't like that at all. She'd based her relationship with him on a lie. He was just better at hiding what he thought than most people.

The truth hurt in ways she couldn't yet define, but this wasn't the time to deal with that. Later, when she was alone, she would curl up and lick her wounds, but not until then. While he was around, she would make sure she stayed strong.

"Let's come at this from a different direction," she said quietly. "Here are the facts. I'm pregnant and you're the father. Honestly, I didn't think you'd have any interest in a child, but I can see I was wrong about that. I'm glad you want to be a part of the baby's life. I'm willing to work with you to come up with some kind of a plan so you can be a part of things. Please understand that I don't want to exclude you at all, but none of this is an invitation for you to move in here with me."

She wasn't going to say anything about his proposal, mostly because she didn't think she could get the words out without her voice cracking and she didn't want Zane to know how much he'd wounded her.

Zane shook his head. "We have to get married."

Not "I love you." Not even "You really matter to me." Just a bald statement of what he saw as fact.

"Why?" she asked.

"It's necessary. A child needs two parents."

"Our baby will *have* two parents."

He frowned. "You know what I mean. Two parents who live together."

"You didn't have that and you turned out fine."

"I want more for our child. I want…" He paced to the window and looked out. "Marry me, Nicki. Just say yes."

If only he knew how much she wanted to agree. She loved him and spending the rest of her life with him was her idea of perfect happiness. But not like this. Not as an obligation. If he'd said he cared, that she mattered, she might have been willing to wait for deep friendship and respect to grow into love. But now she wasn't even sure about that. Did Zane respect her? How much did he care and why?

"No," she whispered.

He turned back to face her. "Then I want to move in."

"No. You have your house and I have this one. When the baby comes—"

He cut her off. "I don't want to wait that long. I want to be a part of things now."

"There's nothing going on. The baby isn't even the size of a rice grain. What do you want to do?"

He shook his head, obviously frustrated. She didn't know what to say, either. Because none of this was what she'd expected for her life. A baby before a husband? That hadn't exactly been her master plan.

He exhaled. "You win, but only for now. I'm not giving up on this."

"Fine. I'm not changing my mind." Not unless he could come to her and tell her he loved her.

He crossed to the front door and let himself out. She watched him go.

When she was finally alone, she covered her face with her hands and gave into the tears again. Nothing about their conversation felt like a victory to her. Instead she was left feeling empty and alone, and in love with a man who was willing to marry her for the sake of a child, but not for herself.

Chapter Twelve

Midmorning Tuesday Zane walked up the front path to Jeff's house. He knew his partner was in an all-day meeting, which was fine. Zane had come here to talk to Ashley.

He knocked on the front door and waited. When she appeared, she had eighteen-month-old Michael on her hip and a sippy cup in her free hand.

"Zane? Hi. What's going on?"

He shrugged. "I just…" He ran his hand through his hair. "I need to talk to you. Is this an okay time?"

"Sure."

She stepped back to let him enter. Zane followed her to the family room where she set Michael on a play mat. There were all kinds of toys surrounding the kid and when he picked up a brightly colored plastic dog, various musical notes blared out.

Ashley offered Zane something to drink, which he

declined. He sat on one end of the sofa, while she settled on the other. She was close enough to Michael that she could offer him a set of baby-size workshop tools.

Zane studied the baby. Michael was sturdy-looking, with sandy-colored hair and hazel eyes. He was a blend of both his parents. Outgoing, bright, friendly. And so damn vulnerable it made Zane break out in a sweat.

He sprang to his feet and walked the length of the large family room. Pictures, toys and books covered all the tables. The room was bright, lived in and felt happy. As if lots of good times happened in this space.

He stopped in front of the sliding glass door and turned back to Ashley. She still sat on the sofa, but her expression had turned from curious to concerned.

"I need to talk," he told her.

"I figured that much out."

"It's just…" He swore silently, not sure how much to tell her. What was she going to think, to say? Did Nicki want people to know? Hell, they would find out eventually.

"I can tell from the track you want to wear out in my carpet that Nicki told you she was pregnant," Ashley said calmly.

Zane stared at her. "You knew?"

"She found out shortly after you two got back from Los Angeles and told me over the weekend." Ashley slid onto the floor and rubbed her son's back. "I told her it was something in the water over there at the office. First Jeff got me pregnant, then you do the same with Nicki." Humor brightened her voice.

"Haven't either of you guys ever heard of condoms? They're these neat latex devices that fit over your—"

He cut her off with a shake of his head. "Yes, I know what a condom is." As for Jeff getting her pregnant, that wasn't anything similar. Jeff had been eighty percent gone before he'd ever slept with Ashley and making love with her had made him fall hard. It had taken Jeff a few weeks to figure out the truth, but Zane had known it all along. This situation was completely different.

"She doesn't understand," he said as he paced to the entertainment center on the far wall. "This was a shock, but I'm dealing with it. The thing is, I want to be there for her. I want to take care of things." He paused and looked at her. "I want to marry her, but she refused. I can't let her do that. I need to be there to keep her safe. And the baby. What about the baby?"

Ashley studied him. "You have it bad."

He did, but not in the way she meant. The fear was with him every second. The past lurked. How the hell was he going to keep it at bay? How was he going to have this turn out differently? He couldn't lose Nicki and their baby—not and survive. Why couldn't she see that?

"Tell me what to do," he said.

"Mother Nature has made sure there's not much you *can* do until the baby is born. Zane, take a deep breath and relax. Nicki is perfectly healthy. There's no reason to think her pregnancy won't progress like millions of others. She'll have good days and bad days. She'll swell up like a balloon and get stretch marks and eat right and take vitamins. In nine months, give or take a few days, she'll give birth. That's when she's going to really need you. But until then, just let nature take its course.''

She wasn't helping. ''How do I get Nicki to marry me? I need to convince her.''

''Why?''

''I have to be there with her. I want to take care of her. I can't do that from fifteen miles away.''

''Not a very good reason to marry someone.''

He knew what she meant. That most couples married for love. Because they cared. Because they wanted to build a life together.

He'd wanted that once—with Amber. He'd seen their future, their kids, their life after the Marines. He'd known he would grow old with her. Right up until the day he killed her.

He sank into a recliner. He couldn't love Nicki. He'd vowed to never love anyone again. He couldn't stand to go through that again. Not ever.

''She's important to me,'' he said at last.

''Wow. Words to warm a woman's heart for sure,'' Ashley told him. ''No wonder she didn't jump at your proposal.'' She pulled Michael onto her lap and stroked his hair.

''Here's the thing, Zane. You have eight-plus months until the baby arrives. Why don't you simply accept Nicki's ground rules for now. Live with them, see if they work. If, as the time for the birth gets closer, you still feel this strongly about getting married, then ask her again. In the meantime, I suggest you look at what's going on and think about whether or not there's a way to be a part of both of their lives without living together. Other couples have made it work.''

He nodded because that was what she expected.

But he hadn't found the information he'd been looking for. The magic sentence that would make Nicki say yes.

He thanked Ashley for her time and left. On his way back to the office, he decided that that he would go into a "wait and see" mode. He would study the situation and look for weaknesses on Nicki's part. There had to be some way to convince her and he would find it. In the meantime, he would do everything in his power to protect her and his unborn child. He was a trained expert. He had skills and he intended to use them.

Nicki pulled the lunch cooler she often brought to work out from under the desk. It was like opening a can of tuna with a hungry cat in the house. Somehow Zane heard the noise from the other side of the office and suddenly appeared in her doorway.

"What are you eating?" he asked.

Before she could answer, he took the container and unzipped the top. As she watched in a combination of amazement, amusement and horror, he laid out her sandwich, the salad she'd made and the piece of fruit. Then he pulled a small notebook from his shirt pocket, flipped it open and noted her choices.

"How much protein on the sandwich?" he asked as he wrote.

She considered the question. "I used a couple of slices of ham."

"Any in the salad? Beans, chicken, cheese?"

"No."

He didn't look happy with her answer. "You're not getting enough protein, Nicki. And don't use lunch meat. You want something more high quality than that.''

"What I want is to be left alone in peace," she told him. "Zane, it's been all of three days and you're driving me crazy. You check on my breakfast. You call me at home to find out what I'm having for dinner."

His dark gaze never left her face. "So?"

"So, it's nuts. I eat a healthy diet about ninety percent of the time. I think that's fine."

He frowned. "Not while you're pregnant. I'm going to Pike Place Market after work. I'll pick up some fresh fish and produce and drop it by."

She knew his heart was in the right place, but if he kept this up, she was going to have to get a restraining order against him. Worse, while he was trying to be caring and supportive, he was breaking her heart about fifteen times a day. Like just now. He'd told her he was buying her food, but he hadn't mentioned anything about staying with her to enjoy it. He didn't seem to want to come over to dinner or talk or anything.

"I should have the food chart ready by then," he said.

She winced. "I thought you were kidding about that."

"No. I'll print out the spreadsheet, seven copies at a time. All you have to do is fill in the foods you eat. The chart will show how many of the various food groups you should have and the quantities. You can pick anything you like within that category."

"How generous," she murmured.

"Your nutritional needs have changed," he said. "And they'll continue to change with each trimester.

Research shows that vital elements of the baby's neurological system are being formed even as we speak.''

Zane had devoured several books on pregnancy in the past couple of days. Nicki was still in the first chapter of the one she'd bought.

''I appreciate the need for good nutrition,'' she said. ''But I'm not sure my doctor expects me to be this regimented.''

As soon as the *D* word passed her lips, she wanted to call it back. Zane slapped the notebook closed and tucked it back in his shirt pocket.

''The appointment is still next Wednesday, right?'' he asked.

She nodded.

''I'll be there.''

Hardly news, she thought. Zane might not have moved in with her, but he was sticking about as close as a tick. Just this morning he'd wanted to talk about her fiber intake. Of course he'd insisted on accompanying her to the doctor. His list of questions had reached two pages.

While Nicki could handle his worries about the baby, it was the other questions she didn't want to hear. Like the ones where he asked the doctor how her disability would impact fetal growth and delivery.

In the past couple of days she'd ceased to be a person to Zane. Instead she was the woman responsible for his baby's gestation.

''Want to come over and watch the game on Saturday?'' she asked. ''The University of Washington is playing UCLA. I'll even give you points.''

He shook his head. ''I would like to meet to discuss future modifications of your exercise program.''

Nicki slammed her hands against the desk. ''Dammit, Zane, back off. I mean it. You're making me crazy with your micromanagement of my life. I'm fine. The baby's fine. Go live your life. If you don't want to hang out with me, then find another bimbo and have at it. I will be your friend, or your lover or both. But I will not be some science experiment. Whatever your problem is, get over it. Do you understand me?''

She'd raised her voice with each sentence so that by the time she finished, she was practically shouting. Her last words echoed in the still room.

For a second she thought she'd gotten through to him. Zane nodded and even gave her a slight smile. But when he spoke, hope died.

''You're starting to feel the mood swings. I read about them. Don't worry, it's just hormones. Things will get more even in your second trimester. As for me backing off, it's not going to happen. You might not understand what's at stake here, but I do. And I'm never going to forget it.''

Nicki spent the weekend trying to figure out how she was going to tell her parents she was pregnant. She knew they would be very excited about being grandparents, but they also had big plans for a wedding. Despite the fact that she'd told them she didn't expect them to pay for her trip down the aisle, they'd been saving for years. Every few months, her mother sent her pictures of bridal dresses or cakes. Just for Nicki to look at.

They loved her, she thought Monday morning as she wheeled through the quiet office and headed for the company gym. They wanted her to be happy. Unfortunately she was about to disappoint them in a huge way.

Oh, they wouldn't say anything. They both adored Zane and would welcome him to the family. But having a baby without first being married wouldn't make them proud.

Although right now her folks were the least of her problems, she thought as she entered the workout room.

"Nicole," Ted called from his place at the chest press. "You're looking especially lovely this morning. Ever consider the value of working out naked?"

The familiar banter with her co-worker eased her tension. She grinned.

"You're a sexist pig, Theodore."

Ted finished with his exercise and sat up. He was tall, muscular and could have squashed her head like a bug. "I like naked women," he said without the least bit of remorse. "So sue me."

"I just might have to do that."

"What if I offered to take my clothes off, too?"

"Nobody wants to see your hairy butt," Rob said as he strolled into the room. "Least of all a classy chick like Nicki. What's going on, kid?"

"I'm good," Nicki said. "Why aren't you in New York with the royals?"

"They headed home. This was all just preliminary work. The real trip starts at the end of the month." Rob headed for the treadmills. He'd tied his long, blond hair back in a ponytail. As he stepped onto the machine, he flipped his towel on the side bar.

"Yup, just me, the princess and the New York skyline."

Nicki laughed. ''Oh, what about her husband? I've heard that El Bahar men are very hot-blooded.''

''You wouldn't want to lose your head,'' Ted joked.

Rob ignored them both and punched in the program on the machine.

Feeling better than she had in a week, Nicki made her way to the recumbent bike and shifted onto the seat. After strapping her feet in place, she started her workout.

There were several programs to choose from on the bike, along with intensity levels and adjustments to time. She punched in her favorite and set the difficulty level for five. After setting the clock for thirty minutes, she began to cycle.

Her muscles were slow to warm up. For the first half mile there were an assortment of aches and pains that finally gave way to a sense of strength. She picked up the pace.

Twelve minutes and thirty-seven seconds into her workout, the door to the gym burst open and Zane stalked in. He looked so annoyed that neither Rob nor Ted called out a greeting. Nicki ran through her activities for the past twelve hours, which was about how long it had been since Zane had checked in with her, and couldn't figure out what rule she could have violated.

She'd eaten a snack before coming in, blending the protein-carb ratio perfectly. She was already into her second eight-ounce glass of water. She had a healthy breakfast waiting for her in her office and...

''Wait just one darn minute,'' she said as Zane stopped next to her. ''You're not my mother. If you can't be pleasant to me and our co-workers then you can leave right now.''

"I'm pleasant," he snarled. He turned to the two bodyguards. "Good morning." It sounded more like an order than a greeting. His attention swung back to her. "You're not wearing a heart monitor."

"What?"

"A heart monitor. I bought you one."

Sure enough he pulled the equipment out of a box and handed it to her.

"Why on earth do I need this?"

He looked at her as if she had an IQ of sixteen. "So I can monitor your heart."

He thrust the band that would wrap around her chest toward her. She took it and stared at the strip of rubber and elastic.

"No way," she said, but Zane was already strapping the display unit on his wrist.

She actually yelped. "You are so kidding," she told him, her temper flaring to the point of spontaneous combustion. "There is no way in hell that you're going to put a heart monitor on me, then keep the display for yourself."

"I'm the one who's interested."

"You're the one who's crazy."

They glared at each other.

In the background she heard scuffling noises. She turned her head and saw both Rob and Ted heading for the door. She knew it was more about them escaping from the fight than any desire to give them privacy.

She returned her attention to Zane, determined to win this battle. He blinked first.

"I really want this, Nicki," he said, his tone slightly more reasonable. "It's important to me."

She could understand that. Respect it even. But not at the price of her privacy and well-being.

"Zane, you have *got* to stop. Women have been having babies since the beginning of time and I'm going to guess almost none of them wore heart monitors. Okay? So back off."

She held out the band. After a couple of seconds, he took it.

"Would you wear it if I let *you* have the display?" he asked.

"No."

He nodded and shoved the unit back in the box, then he turned and left the room.

She was alone. After a couple of seconds, she began peddling again, even though she was no longer in the mood to work out. Everything was different, she thought sadly. Just a couple of weeks ago their time in the gym had been fun and sexy. She and Zane would talk and joke. He helped her with her exercises and she watched his long-legged strength and grace. Now all that was lost.

She missed him. She missed *them*. And she didn't know how to get everything back the way it was.

"Just perfect," Dr. Sheri Grant said with a smile. "I'm going to let you get dressed, then we'll meet in my office. I'm sure you have a lot of questions. I have answers, and some information I'd like to give you."

The poor woman had no idea what she was getting into, Nicki thought as she sat up and watched her doctor leave the examining room. Zane had been surprisingly quiet during the physical examine. After introducing himself, he'd taken a seat in the corner of the room and had simply observed.

Nicki had a feeling that was all going to change when they moved on to the next stage of the appointment. The previous afternoon Zane had given her a typed list of his questions, along with the offer to add hers to his. As he'd come up with things she'd never thought of, she'd done little more than read through the three pages and shake her head.

Now she waited while he came over and lifted her down to her wheelchair.

"I did some research on Dr. Grant," he said while he settled her in place.

"I don't doubt that."

"She's very experienced, well respected and has a pleasant bedside manner, which will be important to you. From what I can tell, she favors open communications with her patients."

Nicki cared less about his recitation than the fact that she wasn't wearing anything but a thin cotton robe. Hadn't Zane noticed her bare skin when he'd lifted her up to the table or back down into her chair? Did he want to pause and feel the warmth of her body so close to his? Didn't he find any of this a turn-on?

Apparently not, as he told her he would wait outside in the hallway while she dressed.

Five minutes later they were in Dr. Grant's office. Zane tried to hand her the small lunch bag he'd brought.

"You should eat something," he told her.

"I'm not hungry." Okay, if she were to tell the absolute truth, she felt a slight gnawing in her stomach, but there was no way she was going to encourage

Zane by taking the food he'd insisted on dragging to their appointment.

"You had breakfast at eight," he said. "It's nearly noon. You need food in your system."

She sighed. "What I need is some quality time with a normal person."

He ignored that. "I have string cheese and some grapes."

He opened the bag just as Dr. Grant stepped into the room. Nicki grabbed the lunch sack and shoved it into her purse.

Dr. Grant, a tall, slender woman in her mid-forties, settled behind her desk.

"New mothers and fathers-to-be always have lots of questions," she said with a smile. "I want to answer all of them. We have plenty of time, so don't be shy. Oh, let me give you this first. I don't want to forget."

She handed over a thick envelope filled with brochures and booklets on everything from weight gain to cloth versus disposable diapers. Nicki took it and pulled out the first sheet while Zane launched into his questions.

"I understand that Nicki will need to take extra vitamins. Now the prenatal variety offer extra supplements, but what about a regimen we put together ourselves? I've done some research—"

At that point he actually pulled out a chart. He had two copies, one of which he passed over to Dr. Grant.

"I've listed the makeup of the three most popular prenatal vitamins currently used. As you can see, the second column lists all known requirements for a pregnant woman. And while we're on the subject of supplements and nutrition, I've been reading about the advantages of more fish for pregnant women.''

Nicki winced.

Dr. Grant sat back and shook her head. ''Zane, did you print out the questions you'd like me to answer?''

''Sure. If you prefer to handle it that way.''

He passed over his multipage list.

She scanned the material. ''I see you're concerned about sleep, exercise. Aha. Oh, imported fruits and vegetables. I don't usually get asked that one.''

Nicki looked at him. ''When did you add that?''

''Last night. There was something on the news about the fact that we're getting close to winter. Soon our fruits and vegetables will be coming from the southern hemisphere. Is that all right?''

''Of course it's all right,'' she snapped. ''If not for those imports, we wouldn't see so much as a grape until spring. You are *not* keeping me from eating fruit for this entire pregnancy.''

''Of course I want you to eat fruit. That's the point.'' He turned back to the doctor. ''You understand my concern.''

''Of course.'' Dr. Grant read off a few more items. ''Is it all right for Nicki to be in the house while the cleaning service is there? What about exercise? Oh, I see you've included her workout schedule.'' She smiled at Zane. ''You're very thorough.''

''You have no idea,'' Nicki muttered.

''I do. I've seen this before.'' Her expression turned sympathetic. ''The good news is it gets better.''

Zane didn't look pleased to be discussed in this way. ''What gets better?''

''The obsession,'' Dr. Grant said. ''You want to do

everything in your power to keep Nicki and the baby safe.''

Zane stiffened. ''How did you know?''

''It's not an uncommon reaction. Especially for a first-time father. You're not physically a part of the baby the way Nicki is. You're excited, terrified and want to put Nicki in a plastic bubble to keep her from harm. The baby, too, of course.''

Zane didn't look convinced. ''It's not that simple.''

''I understand.'' She set the list on her desk. ''Zane, Nicki is healthy, you're healthy, there's no reason to think this pregnancy will be anything but completely normal. Monitoring every detail of her life isn't going to change anything, but it will increase her stress level. You think you're helping, but in this case, you're creating a problem where one doesn't exist.''

Nicki reached out and touched his arm. ''She's right. I want you to be a part of things, but you can't monitor every speck of food I put into my mouth.''

He looked as if he wanted to ask why not. She supposed that she could see his point. His job was to keep people safe. Of course he would feel that more intensely about his child. If she were in—

She froze in her chair as her brain clicked over a few important pieces of information. Zane's list of questions. The ones that had embarrassed her and frustrated her and made her want to shake him were all about her health. What she was eating, how much she was sleeping, vitamins. Nothing on those pages was about her being in a wheelchair. He'd never mentioned it even once.

She shook her head and called herself fifteen kinds of idiot. Zane hadn't been lying when he said it didn't matter and she hadn't believed him. Because it was the easiest place to go. Talk about dumb.

She wanted to take a few minutes to dwell on her realization but this wasn't the time. However, the information did give her the impetus to see things from his point of view.

"How about if we make a deal," she said. "You can monitor me until you start to make me crazy. I'll make a serious effort to be patient and you'll promise to back off when I tell you to. Then we'll see how it goes and hope Dr. Grant is right, and that this will all calm down in a month or two."

Zane looked from her to the doctor.

"It sounds like a plan to me," Dr. Grant said.

Zane nodded slowly. "All right. As long as you agree to eat more quality protein."

She thought about the three pounds of salmon he'd left in her refrigerator. "I'll do my best."

"Okay."

Dr. Grant smiled at them both. "All right. Now let me answer a few of the more 'normal' questions."

She reviewed the workout schedule. "Nicki, all this is fine. You may experience some days when you're more tired, so go easy if that feels right. None of your workout is weight-bearing so you won't have to change it as you get closer to term. You're biggest problem will be dealing with your increasing midsection. I'm sure Zane can help you modify your routine when the time comes."

"That would be great," she said.

Zane agreed.

"There are going to be a few considerations due to you being in a wheelchair," her doctor continued. "As you don't use your legs walking around, I want you to get in the habit of putting your feet up a few times a day. This will help with circulation.''

''You're thinking of blood clots,'' Zane said. ''I read about them.''

''I'm sure you did.'' Dr. Grant looked at him. ''This is preventative, There's no indication that Nicki is going to have a problem.''

''I understand.'' He turned to Nicki. ''I could build something for under your desk. If it was the right height and placement, you could stretch out your legs while still in your chair.''

''Perfect,'' she said, equally annoyed and amused. He cared, she reminded herself. Maybe he didn't love her, but wasn't his obsessive worry a twisted sign of affection? It beat not caring at all.

''All other daily activities are fine,'' Dr. Grant said. ''Including the one that got you into my office in the first place. Some couples worry that making love will hurt the baby. That's not the truth. Most couples find that their intimacy is more special in pregnancy. It will bond the two of you, which you're going to need to survive the 2:00 a.m. feedings.''

Nicki found herself unable to look at Zane. Ever since he found out about her pregnancy he'd been a whole lot less interested in her as a person. She couldn't imagine him ever wanting to make love with her again.

But she wanted to, very much. She thought about their times together, how he'd made her feel, how she'd wanted to please him, and she missed it.

Did he? Did he think about those nights and wish for more? She sighed. One day very soon she was going to have to find the courage to ask him. And if the answer was yes, then she was going to have to do whatever it took to get him back into her bed.

Chapter Thirteen

On the way back to the office, Zane thought about what had happened at the appointment. He knew Dr. Grant lumped him in with all the other neurotic fathers-to-be and there was no way he could explain the truth about his past. But one piece of information *had* caught his attention. That his overmonitoring of Nicki's health would cause her more stress, which would have a physical impact on her body.

Which meant he was going to have to be more subtle in his approach.

He glanced over at her. She sat behind the steering wheel, her attention on the road. When they stopped for a traffic light, he spoke.

"I'm going to back off," he said.

She turned toward him and raised her eyebrows. "I'm not sure I believe you."

He nearly smiled. Damn, but she knew him well.

"I'm going to *try* to back off. Maybe shoot for twenty percent."

"It's a start."

The light turned green and she eased the van forward.

"I'll try to be more cooperative about some things, too," she said. "Like when I work out, I'll put on the heart monitor, but *I* get to wear the display unit. Fair enough?"

He nodded. He didn't care who wore it, as long as she kept track of her heart rate. Scratch that. He *did* care, but he was willing to let this one go.

"I'd like to read through the material when you're done with it," he said.

"Okay. I'll look it all over this weekend and bring it to work on Monday." She sighed. "Speaking of work, we're going to have to make an announcement at some point. We've both been acting weird, so I'm guessing everyone knows something is up, even if they don't have specifics. And in time, my condition will become obvious to everyone."

He hadn't thought about that. About people knowing. He and Amber had never reached that stage. When she'd died, he decided not to burden her family further by telling them she'd been pregnant.

"What about your folks?" he asked.

"Not something I want to think about."

"They want grandkids," he told her. "They'll be happy."

"They're more into the traditional way of doing things, and don't remind me that you've offered to marry me. I'm aware of that."

He wanted to make his case again, to tell her it was

the only way to make things work, but he held back. For now.

"I can't decide if I should tell them over the phone or wait until they come up for Thanksgiving," she continued. "That's two months from now, and they might not understand why I waited so long. But they're heading out to Australia any day now, so that's a good excuse to keep things quiet for a while."

"I could tell them," he offered.

She glanced at him. "You were a marine, weren't you. Talk about stepping into enemy fire." She lowered her voice. "Hi, Mr. and Mrs. Beauman. I'm calling to let you know I knocked up your only daughter."

"I wouldn't phrase it like that."

"There are very few delicate ways to tell my parents I'm pregnant. Believe me, I've been trying to find one or two."

He felt helpless and hated the feeling. If she would just marry him, this problem, along with several others, would be solved.

She turned left at the signal, then pulled into the office parking lot.

"Thanks for coming with me, Zane."

He stared at her. "I thought you didn't want me to go with you, but you didn't know how to stop me."

She smiled. "That was true at first. But you didn't ask any embarrassing questions during the actual exam and I liked not being alone."

Suddenly he wanted to touch her. Not just to take her pulse or see if she had a fever, but because he ached for her. There was an emptiness inside him that only Nicki seemed to fill.

"I want to come to all your appointments."

"I know. I guess I'm going to let you." She pulled the keys out of the ignition. "And while we're on the subject of you helping out, I want to redo one of the bedrooms at my place. You know, paint, maybe a border print. Do you want to help?"

"Of course."

"Good, because I bought a crib and I've tried to put it together and it's just not happening."

He grinned. "You might be a computer whiz, but you're lousy with a screwdriver."

"I do okay. But the directions make no sense. I can't tell what part is what and none of them fit together right."

"I'll take a look at it. What are you doing Saturday?"

She shrugged. "Hanging out."

"How about if I pick up some paint chips and swing by? I'll work on the crib while you pick out colors."

"Works for me. There's a wallpaper store by me. Maybe I'll stop on my way home and borrow some sample books. We can look at border prints together."

"There are no words to describe my joy."

She laughed and for that second, some of the fear left Zane. They were what they had always been— good friends who cared about each other. Then he remembered about the baby and everything was different again. Everything but one.

Even though he knew it was dangerous, even though he knew it would distract him from his main mission of keeping her safe, the wanting had returned and he didn't know how to make it go away.

* * *

Zane showed up late Saturday morning. Nicki let him in, then laughed when she saw the bags, boxes and charts he carried.

"We're talking about getting a room ready for a baby, not planning an invasion of a third world country."

"Paint chips," he said as he set down a bag filled with a rainbow of bits of color. "My toolbox so I can put the crib together. The additional wallpaper books you asked me to pick up because the eight you had weren't enough, and graph paper so we can lay out the room to scale and plan where the furniture will go."

She closed the door behind him. "Of course. Graph paper. And me without a scrap in the house. What *was* I thinking?"

He gave her a mock glare.

Nicki waved toward the kitchen. "I made coffee. Help yourself." Before he could start in on her, she shook her head. "It's a fresh pot I made just for you. I already had my cup of decaf, thank you very much."

"Thanks," he said as he walked down the hall.

Nicki picked up the bag with the paint chips and carried it into the living room. She dumped the contents onto her low coffee table and started sorting through the options.

There were single color chips, strips with a dark color at each end—one flat, one gloss—with a white tint in the middle, and chips with five samples ranging from light to dark in that color family. Right away she noticed a definite theme.

When Zane walked into the living room, she turned to him. "These are nearly all blue."

"No way. There are other colors."

She searched through the pile. "I found one pink chip, three green and a handful of yellows. Are you hoping for a boy?"

He shrugged, looking more than a little sheepish. "I thought it would be fun to have a son."

"Let me guess. You're thinking sports and cars. If we have a daughter, you're going to have to learn to do the hair ribbon thing. And take her to dance class."

He barely kept from shuddering. "I couldn't do that."

"We're going to have to talk about that at some point," she said.

He sat on the sofa and picked up a blue paint chip. "Dance class?"

"The sex of the baby," she said. "Do we want to know in advance?"

Zane looked at her. "From the ultrasound."

She nodded. "I haven't decided yet. There's a part of me that says there are too few real surprises in life and that it would add to the excitement not to know. My more practical nature says if we know, we can plan the room better."

"I don't know, either."

Nicki had a feeling that his indecision came from other concerns, such as would he protect her better if he knew or if he didn't know. She wished she understood what was going on inside his head and why he was so freaked out about the whole thing. She'd honestly expected panic and indifference, not this burning desire to run her life.

Although she had to admit that he'd backed off as promised. When he'd called the previous evening to check on her, he hadn't even asked what she'd had for dinner. Of course she'd heard the tension in his voice, so she'd taken pity on him and had offered the information.

"Do you need more paint chips?" he asked. "I can get different colors."

"These are fine. I was thinking of yellow anyway. It's a cheery color on our gray days."

"Once you pick out what you want, I'll do the work."

She rolled her eyes. "Because using a brush and roller will strain me in my delicate condition?"

"Because I don't want you breathing in the fumes."

"Okay. Good point. I'll let you do the painting." She smiled. "You're going to have to do the border print anyway. I can't reach."

"Not a problem." He glanced at his coffee mug, then at her. "You don't have to keep telling me what you're eating. I'm going to let that go."

"Really? Even if I have ice cream?"

He looked distressed, but instead of complaining said, "I'd like you to eat right about eighty percent of the time."

"That's what I want to do, Zane." She rolled close to him and touched his arm. "I'm nervous about this whole baby thing, too. I want to stay as healthy as possible. Even if I get the occasional craving for a chili cheeseburger."

"You'll want to pass on that."

"Why? Too much fat?"

"You'll get heartburn. Pregnant women are more susceptible."

"That's romantic," she grumbled.

He tugged on a lock of hair. "I live to serve. Come on. Show me the crib."

She led him into one of the spare bedrooms. She'd chosen the one that faced south for the baby's room, so it would get plenty of light in the winter, but not be too hot in the summer. A partially assembled crib lay in pieces on the floor.

Zane crouched down and picked up a railing. "This isn't new."

"Oh. Didn't I mention it was an antique? That's why I bought it. A woman brought it in to sell on consignment while I was looking around the baby furniture store. The salesperson didn't want to take it, but I was interested. The woman had a picture of what it looked like and when I saw that, I fell in love with it."

She pointed to the old photograph she'd tacked up on the wall.

"Where are the instructions?" he asked.

She glanced around at the pieces. "Over there. By the headboard. Or is it a footboard."

Zane picked them up and frowned. "They're handwritten."

"I know. Isn't it cool? I thought I'd put the crib together and make sure all the parts were there, then take it apart and strip it down and either stain or paint it."

He groaned. "You don't even know if all the pieces are here?"

"The woman said they were, but there's only one way to tell."

"And you didn't want to buy something out of a box because why?"

"I want it to be special. I love that this crib is nearly a hundred years old."

"Yeah, that's real exciting. Do you see how close together the rails are? Do you know how much work that's going to be to strip?"

"Honestly, I haven't a clue."

"Great."

She couldn't help smiling. "If it's too much trouble I could hire someone to—"

He cut her off with a growl. "Fine. I'll get it together, then take it apart and strip it down. When do you plan to decide about paint versus stain."

"I have no idea."

He looked at her. "You're being difficult on purpose, aren't you?"

"Maybe just a little. To pay you back."

He grunted. "Sit tight," he said as he rose. "I'll be right back."

He returned with several brochures for dressers, changing tables and bassinets. "I've been doing some research."

"Of course you have."

He ignored that. "Babies need a lot of stuff. Most of it is a standard height."

He opened one brochure and set it on her lap, then crouched next to her.

"See the changing table?" he asked, pointing. "It's going to be too high for you. The dresser is less of a problem, but the top drawer can still be difficult."

She nodded but didn't speak. She wasn't sure where he was going with this.

"So I talked with this buddy of mine," he told her. "He does a lot of custom work. I explained the problem, how you'd need the table low and I'd want it to be the regular height. He came up with this.''

Zane pulled a folded piece of paper out of the back pocket of his jeans and passed it to her.

''See this lever here? It will raise and lower the table to different preset heights. You'd just lift it or lower it. These steel pins would lock into place, so we wouldn't have to worry about the table shifting while the baby was on it. He told me that he'd be happy to match whatever style we want.'' He shrugged. ''If you're interested.''

Nicki looked from the sketch to Zane. Deep inside, something cold and frozen warmed enough to melt. Her heart fluttered a little.

This was the Zane she'd fallen for. The man who thought of her being in a wheelchair as little more than a fact of life. Whatever logistical problems it presented were simply challenges to be solved, nothing more. He didn't judge her. She'd been wrong to think he did. Funny how all these years after she'd made peace with her condition, that was still the first place she went when something went wrong. Apparently the healing took a whole lot longer than she'd realized.

''I think it's a brilliant idea,'' she told him. ''You were really sweet to think of this.''

He looked at her, his dark eyes filled with concern. ''You sure I'm not stepping on your toes?''

She wiggled her bare feet. ''Not even close.''

''Good.''

He sat on the floor and picked up a piece of the crib. ''At least we have a long time until the kid is going to have to use this.''

''What? You can storm beaches and overthrow

governments but you can't put together one little bitty crib?''

He collected a handful of screws and shook his head. ''I'll have to get back to you on that.''

She watched him sort through the parts. As always, he moved with a graceful ease that left her breathless. Wanting stirred deep inside. Wanting and a need to connect with him. She missed the intimacy they'd shared. Not just the lovemaking, but the friendship. From what she could tell, they were taking baby steps in that direction. How long until they were back where they had been a couple of weeks ago? Or was that lost forever?

''Do you think I'll be a good mother?'' she asked.

Zane looked at her. ''Of course. Why?''

''I worry. I've never been a parent before. I don't want to mess up the kid.''

''Your parents did a good job with you, so you've seen how it should be done.''

''I hadn't thought of that,'' she told him.

''I've been reading that they think intelligence is passed down through the mother. So the baby will be smart.''

That made her smile. ''How comforting. Now if only he or she will inherit your mechanical abilities.''

He glanced at the pieces he held. ''I'll get it.''

''I have no doubt.''

Zane knew she didn't. Nicki trusted him with a completeness that left him humble. And terrified. He couldn't believe she worried about being a good mother. She was patient, loving, funny. She knew what it was like to be part of a family. What did he know? He'd grown up on the streets. He'd belonged to a gang, which wasn't exactly like being a part of mainstream society.

He'd agreed to back off the monitoring, which intellectually he knew was the right thing, but in his gut, he sweated every second of every day.

A thousand things could go wrong. Didn't she see that? If he was around, he could protect her. He could save her—which he hadn't been able to do with Amber.

"We're going to have to talk about names, too," Nicki said. "I know this is way premature, but I suspect we're going to argue about it, so we may want to start that early."

"Because you love a good fight?" he asked.

"So I'll have more time to convince you that I'm right."

She laughed as she spoke. This morning she wore her hair loose. There wasn't much makeup on her face, but her cheeks glowed with color. She was so beautiful, it was almost painful to look at her.

Dressing for the unseasonably warm fall day, she'd pulled on shorts and a sleeveless T-shirt. He could see the perfect lines of her body. He thought her breasts might be a little fuller, but otherwise, there weren't any physical manifestations of her condition that he could see.

Still, the baby grew inside of her. His baby. Their baby.

He dropped the crib pieces on the floor and shifted onto his knees. Cupping her face in his hands, he stared into her eyes.

"Marry me," he breathed.

Her green eyes darkened with what looked like pain. "I can't."

"Why not?"

"Because you want to control me and I want to be loved."

He dropped his hands as if they'd been burned. Love. Had she really spoken the word?

"I care about you," he said.

The corners of her mouth curved up. "I'm glad."

It wasn't enough. He could see that. But how could he convince her?

"I can't be with anyone else," he told her. "Going out with Heather was a disaster. I thought about you the whole time." He swallowed. "I don't *want* to be with anyone else."

She stroked his cheek with her fingertips. "What happened, big guy? You discover that you need a little conversation while you're doing the wild thing?"

"Yeah."

"I'm glad."

She looked deep into his eyes, as if searching for something. Zane had a bad feeling she wasn't going to find what she wanted. So he did the only thing that made sense. He kissed her.

Chapter Fourteen

What started out as a distraction quickly turned into something else. The second Zane's mouth brushed hers, he found himself caught up in a passion he couldn't control. Need flooded him, making him hard and ready in less than a heartbeat.

He swept his tongue across her lower lip and when she opened for him, he plunged inside. She tasted sweet and hot and he couldn't resist her. Not when she strained toward him, moaning in the back of her throat.

Heat exploded. He wrapped his arms around her and drew her from the chair. When she was on his lap, he slid his hand up her rib cage to her breasts and cupped the luscious curves.

"Yes," she breathed as he lightly touched her already tight nipples. "Oh, Zane, that feels so good."

He'd read that a pregnant woman's breasts could

become more sensitive in the first trimester. He'd thought it would mean that Nicki could find his touch painful. Apparently in her case it just meant she was more erotically responsive. He was man enough not to mind.

He pulled off her T-shirt, unfastened her bra, then bent low to take her nipple in his mouth. As his lips closed around the taut flesh, she sank her nails into his back.

"Oh, yes," she gasped. "I can't believe it. More. Do it more."

She clung to him, panting, pleading, writhing. He sucked a little harder, flicking his tongue against her, and she shuddered.

"It's not possible," she breathed, then shuddered again.

His mind raced. Was she climaxing?

He ripped off his own shirt and laid it on the floor, then lowered her to the soft cotton. Her eyes were unfocused, her mouth slightly parted. He bent down to her breasts again.

At the first brush of his tongue, she sucked in a breath. When he closed his lips around her nipple, she grabbed his head with both hands and held him firmly in place.

He reached for the waistband of her shorts and unfastened the button. After lowering the zipper, he slipped his hand under her panties and headed south. She parted her legs and moaned.

She was damp, he thought as he eased between folds of swollen flesh. Timing the movement of his mouth with the progress of his hand, he slid a finger inside of her just as he drew deeply on her breast.

Strong muscles convulsed around him. Stunned, he moved in and out of her. She sighed her pleasure.

Zane swore and jerked off her shorts and panties, then shoved down his jeans and briefs and pushed into her.

She climaxed with each thrust. He'd never experienced such intense pleasure. The combination of heat, tightness and rippling massage made short work of his control. In an effort to please her as much as possible before he completely lost control, he raised up slightly and slipped a hand between them.

As he rubbed that swollen point of pleasure, she actually screamed. Her entire body surrendered. It was too much for him. He pumped in twice more, then lost control in an explosion of glorious release.

''The problem with doing it on the floor,'' Nicki said a couple of minutes later, ''is that there's no lingering.'' She sighed with satisfaction, then admitted, ''My back is starting to hurt.''

Zane raised his head and smiled. ''Then we'll have to move to the bed.''

She couldn't think of a place she would rather be. ''You just want a repeat performance.''

He kissed her, then sat up and drew her into a sitting position. ''Are you kidding? You were climaxing with me just touching your breasts. Who knows what you're capable of if I put my mind to it.''

She didn't know, either, but the thought of finding out was delightful.

''What about all the work we had planned?'' she asked as he picked her up and carried her into the bedroom.

He lowered her onto the mattress and kissed her.

"Tomorrow," he whispered. "Let's just spend today in bed."

"I'd like that a lot."

"We can even order take-out."

"Chinese?" she asked.

"Whatever you'd like."

Monday morning Nicki practically floated to work. The past two days had been perfect. Zane had gone home Saturday afternoon to pick up a few things, but aside from that, they'd spent every second together.

They'd talked, they'd laughed, they'd made love. Given her body's new delicious sensitivity, the latter had been exquisitely wonderful.

Now as she parked her van and waited for Zane to pull up beside her, she knew that what they'd experienced over the past two days was available to them for the rest of their lives. But only if they both had the courage to fight for it.

Nicki figured she would be the one to start the battle. She loved Zane and she wanted him to love her. For some reason he couldn't...or wouldn't, and she was going to have to find out which. Any attempts she'd made to discuss his past had been skillfully diverted, so she was on her own. Fortunately, she had some ideas and she planned to put them into effect that morning.

"How can I help you?" Jeff asked when she rolled into his office shortly after eleven.

"I need your help with some research."

Jeff smiled. "I'm surprised. You're the best."

"This is a special project. I want to find out about Zane's past."

Her boss's expression didn't change, but she sensed his withdrawal from the conversation.

"This is important," she told him quickly, before he could speak. "I don't know how much Ashley has shared with you, but I'm pregnant. Zane's the father. I'm in love with him, but while he wants to be a part of my life, he's not interested in sharing much more than responsibilities and duties. I want to know why."

Jeff was a pro. She had a feeling he hadn't known about her condition or her relationship with his partner, but not so much as a muscle twitched. His expression remained as it had been.

"Ask him," he said.

"He's not big on chatting about the past."

"Maybe there's a good reason for that."

"I'm sure there is, but that doesn't change my need to know. Why does he hold his heart so carefully out of reach?"

Jeff leaned back in his chair. "Nicki, you're a great employee and a friend. I respect you and I want to help, but Zane is also a friend."

She'd been afraid of this, but she'd had to try. "You're not going to tell me anything, are you?"

"I'll tell you what you're going to find out in your search, and I'll tell you something he hasn't told me but that I've experienced myself."

Jeff rose and crossed to the window. "Zane was in the Marines. We've never discussed his work in detail. I don't know where he was stationed, what he saw, what he knows. But I've seen the same sort of fighting. The death and suffering. It changes a man forever."

"The dark soul of a warrior," she murmured.

Jeff looked at her and raised his eyebrows. She shrugged.

"Ashley mentioned it once," she said. "That there were things in your past that she could never understand. She said you wouldn't share them with her because knowing them would fundamentally change who she is and you didn't want to burden her with that."

"Very true. Soldiers learn to disconnect. To focus on what needs to be done to the exclusion of everything else. In some ways, to be like a machine."

She heard the words, but couldn't reconcile them with what she knew about Zane. He was always joking and teasing. Jeff, on the other hand, was far more intense. Was that difference a reflection of their personalities? Or had they each picked a different way to deal with the past.

"You're saying that Zane has closed himself off," she said. "It's a survival mechanism and once turned on there may not be a way to turn it off?"

"It's a possibility."

"You were able to readjust. You're married, with a family."

He smiled. "I had the help of an extraordinary woman to guide me back to the land of the living. She didn't love me into changing. Instead, by loving her, I was able to see the possibilities."

Was the same opportunity available to Zane? If she hung in there long enough and he allowed himself to care, would he be transformed?

"That's what I know about myself and speculate may be true for Zane," Jeff said as he returned to his chair. "The other piece of information I have is what you'll find when you begin your search. He was married and his wife died. This was about five years ago. She was also a marine.''

Nicki stared at her boss. She couldn't breathe, nor could she feel anything but unexpected pain. It was as if someone had taken a sledgehammer to her heart.

"Married?" she whispered.

Jeff nodded. "I'm sorry, Nicki. I know this is a surprise."

She couldn't believe it. "He never said anything."

"He doesn't talk about it to me much, either. He first mentioned her when I was within inches of being a complete moron and walking away from Ashley. Zane told me not to do it. When I pointed out he was hardly in a position to give romantic advice, he mentioned the woman from his past. Later, at the wedding, he took me aside and told me that there were few joys in life that matched those found in a happy marriage."

"I see."

The words were difficult to force out of her tight throat. She felt cold, stiff and sick to her stomach. The room started to spin and had she been standing, she would have crumpled to the ground.

"Thank you," she whispered. "I have a place to start."

"Are you all right?"

She forced herself to nod. "A little surprised, but I'll get over it."

Jeff leaned toward her. "Nicki, I think Zane is worth fighting for. He cares about you. We can all see it. This may take time, but don't give up. If there's anything I can do…"

"You're being very kind," she said as she turned and wheeled out of his office.

It took every ounce of strength she possessed to get back to her office. Once there, she closed the door and gave into the tears that burned her eyes.

Married! He'd been married. He'd loved someone else. He'd met her, been intrigued, dated her, proposed, then married her. They'd lived together, made plans. He'd touched her, made love with her and mourned her when she died.

Nicki couldn't stand to think about it. She'd thought something had happened to make Zane incapable of loving, but maybe it was just he didn't want to love her.

When the emotional storm had passed, all that was left was the hollowness in her chest. Two sides of her brain battled. Her logical half told her that a man who had loved once could love again. Her emotional side said to give up on what could never be and plan her life without him.

The problem with that last bit of advice was that she was still desperately in love with him. Hadn't she promised herself she wouldn't give up without a fight?

Besides, there was more going on than she realized. Zane's reaction to her pregnancy had been surprising. He hadn't been excited or upset or anything but determined to keep her safe. For the first time, she wondered why. What had happened in his past to make him the way he was?

Jeff had said he thought Zane had been married about five years ago. How had his wife died and was that the reason he couldn't allow himself to connect?

She only knew one way to find out.

* * *

It was nearly seven that evening when Zane walked into her office.

"I thought we agreed you weren't going to work late," he said as he took the chair on the other side of her desk. "It's called a compromise."

He smiled as he spoke. Nicki studied him greedily, as if she had to memorize everything about him. The shape of his eyes, the curve of his cheeks, the way his mouth moved when he talked. She wanted to snuggle up next to him and breathe in his scent. She wanted to love him, and she wanted him to love her back. Unfortunately she was no closer to making that happen than she had been before.

"I had something come up," she said, pulling a handful of sheets off the printer and stacking them with the rest.

"What?"

"I'm trying to break into military records. It's not easy."

He frowned. "It's not only tough, it's illegal. What's going on? Jeff would never give you an assignment like that."

"You're right. I gave this one to myself." She shoved the stack of papers toward him. "Tell me, Zane. What is it, because I sure as hell can't find it. Tell me the secret. Tell me if there's any hope."

"What are you talking about?"

"You."

Nicki knew she was acting out of desperation, but she didn't know where else to turn. She had to know—even if the truth destroyed her and burned away any hope.

"Tell me why you can't love me," she said quietly. "We're so good together. We laugh, we talk. We like the same sports, we argue about politics, we're good in bed. I know you want me—I've seen the proof. But that's not the same as loving me. So what is it? The color of my hair? The scent of my skin? The sound of my voice?'' She swallowed. ''Is it the wheelchair?''

He swore and grabbed the papers. ''What the hell have you been doing?''

''Searching out your past. I want to know why and I can't find it there, so you're going to have to tell me.''

He scanned a couple of sheets, then tossed them back at her. ''It's not the damn chair and you know it.''

''I was pretty sure, but all the women you've dated have been physically perfect and I'm not.'' She wheeled out from behind the desk and banged her hand against the metal frame of her chair. ''This is a part of me. I am not defined by what I can and cannot do, yet it influences who I am. In some ways, I'm a much stronger person. But I can't walk or dance or run. Is that any part of it?''

''No. never.'' He shoved his chair back and stood, glaring at her. ''It's none of that.''

''Then is it about the woman you married?''

He turned away. For a second she thought he might leave, but he didn't. Instead he sank back in the chair and rubbed his eyes.

''Yes. It's about Amber.''

Amber. Nicki froze. Somehow hearing the name made the other woman more real.

''Tell me,'' she whispered.

''You don't want to know.''

"Maybe not, but I need to hear why you won't give us a chance."

He was silent for a long time. She was determined to wait him out. He was right. She didn't *want* to hear the words, but she sensed there was power in the truth.

"We couldn't have been more different," he said quietly, not looking at her but at some point on the wall behind her. "She was from a big family in the south. I was a street kid. But there was something between us from the first. I never expected her to say yes when I asked her out, but she accepted and that was it. By the second date, I was hooked."

The pain was like sharp blades cutting through her body. Nicki felt the cold steel sliding between bone and organs. Her chest constricted, her fingers were numb.

"When I met her folks, I was sure they'd take her aside and tell her it was a big mistake to hang out with me, but they didn't. They made me feel welcome. It was Christmas, and after dinner we went for a walk and I proposed. We were married that spring."

Zane leaned forward and rested his forearms on his thighs. "She was the first woman I'd ever loved. I didn't know how I'd gotten so lucky. She was tough, but feminine. Small, but feisty. We were assigned to an island near the Philippines. We worked together and it was great. Then one day she told me she was pregnant."

Nicki hadn't seen that one coming. It wasn't possible for her to feel more pain, so she simply endured the violent ripping of her dreams. Pregnant. There was nothing she could offer Zane that he hadn't already had with Amber. She was little more than second best.

"I wanted her to go home," he continued. "I was scared that she might get hurt out there and I wanted her to go stateside. She disagreed. She wanted to stay as long as possible. I held the trump card. Once her commanding officer knew she was pregnant, he would send her home. I told her if she didn't come clean, I would do it for her. So she agreed. She packed up and left."

He drew in a breath. "I stood right there while she got on the helicopter. I waved goodbye and yelled that I loved her. I was due to get reassigned in about four months, so I figured we would be together then. I'd be home for the birth of our child."

Nicki knew he was about to tell her something bad. She wanted to stop him, but knew she had to know—even if the telling hurt them both.

"The helicopter rose up toward the sky. As it moved forward, something happened. A mechanical failure. It lurched, then slammed into the side of a mountain. There was an explosion. I remember standing there, feeling the heat on my face. I couldn't move, couldn't speak. I sure as hell couldn't save her. I was the one who had insisted on her getting on that helicopter. I killed her, and the baby."

Nicki didn't know what to say. She couldn't have imagined anything like this.

"That's why I date those other women," he said, raising his head and staring at her. "Because they could never matter. I only ever wanted to love Amber."

The darkness in his eyes made her back up a few feet.

''Of course,'' she whispered. ''None of this was about me being in a wheelchair. It wasn't about me at all.''

She was little more than a bit player in a story that had nothing to do with her. Why couldn't she have seen that before she'd fallen in love with a man who was still in love with a ghost?

Chapter Fifteen

Nicki didn't actually watch Zane leave her office. When he'd finished his story, she turned away, fighting for control. When she'd finally looked back at the chair, he was gone.

Maybe it was better. What was there to say in all this? She'd wanted to know why he wouldn't love her, wouldn't give them a chance, and now she had the information. He was in love with someone else. He always had been.

She felt cold and empty, but worse, she felt ashamed. She'd been so damn sure that she was strong and capable and in charge of her life, but at the first sign of trouble with Zane, she'd assumed it was about her being in a wheelchair. She'd emotionally hidden behind her circumstances because it was easy and convenient. She'd never stopped to consider that it might not be about that at all, which meant she wasn't as far along the road to recovery as she thought.

That wasn't going to make dealing with Zane any easier. Because she was going to have to deal with him. They were having a baby together.

She rubbed her temples and told herself she would survive this. Somehow she would be strong, because she'd been to hell and back and nothing could defeat her. Not even the realization that she'd been wishing after the moon all this time.

She'd thought there was something wrong with him. That he was just afraid of commitment or that he'd been burned by love. She'd even allowed herself to consider the possibility that he was secretly in love with her, but afraid to admit it. But no.

He was in love with his late wife. Maybe he was one of those people who could only love once. A one-woman man. Which left her exactly nowhere. Because no matter how much she didn't want it to be true, she still loved him and she wanted him to love her back.

But she couldn't make him, nor could she change the past. At the end of the day she was alone and forever linked with someone who wouldn't see her as more than a friend he liked to sleep with.

"The death threats against Mr. Sabotini have escalated," Jeff said three days later at the staff meeting. "We're going to coordinate with a multinational task force." He nodded at Nicki. "You'll be spending a lot of time at your computer until this one is resolved."

She looked up from her notes. "Not a problem. I'm already coordinating with our team in New York.

When he brings his family over here, that's their point of entry. Fortunately they'll be flying a private jet and not commercial. That should cut down on some of the risk.''

"Good. My contacts in Europe tell me the clues are mounting, but so far there's not enough for them to move on," Jeff continued.

Nicki wrote down the pertinent information. While she was sorry that Mr. Sabotini and his family were in danger, she appreciated having something to occupy her mind. The intense work situation kept her from thinking about Zane and what a fool she'd been.

It wasn't just finding out that he wouldn't ever love her, it was the loss of him from her life. Gone were the easy lunches, the teasing conversation. He no longer asked about her protein intake or monitored her morning exercise. Since he'd confessed his past, he'd barely spoken to her.

Now they sat at opposite ends of the table, on opposite sides. She was careful not to look in his direction and figured he was probably doing the same. Their co-workers had noticed. Brenda, Jeff's assistant, had stopped by that morning to ask what was up with Zane.

Nicki had pretended ignorance, then had felt like slime for lying. She wasn't eating, wasn't sleeping and knew she had to find a way to function, for the sake of the baby, if not for herself.

The meeting adjourned. As usual, Nicki waited until the room was empty before rolling out into the hallway. Zane was one of the first ones out the door.

As she stared after him, she wondered what she should do. Give up? That plan made the most sense. He loved someone else, which she could handle if he also wanted to love her. But he didn't. Maybe he couldn't, maybe he wasn't interested. She would probably never know. The most sensible course of action was to figure out a way to get over him.

Last night she'd made a list of her options. She could stay where she was and hope for the best. She could quit and find another job in Seattle. Or she could move.

Her parents hadn't been subtle in their hinting that she head down to Tucson. With her degree and her work experience, she knew she wouldn't have trouble finding a job. She might even be able to do something from home. Of course moving would mean that Zane wouldn't be much of a part of his child's life.

She headed for her office. As she settled behind her desk, she considered that. Was it fair to take the baby away from him?

Did he care about the baby?

Nicki leaned back in her chair. Did he? He was worried about her health. He wanted to keep them both safe. He'd made logistical plans about changing tables and dressers, but what about plans to read to their child? To play with it, nurture it? He couldn't get over loving and losing Amber enough to love another woman. Could he get over the child he'd lost to care about the one she carried?

She could accept loving a man who didn't love her back, but she wouldn't subject her baby to that. Not ever. Which might make the decision to leave Seattle a very simple one.

Zane paced in his house. He was exhausted, but knew he didn't want to sleep. Not when the nightmares had returned.

They were vivid, cruel and detailed. In them he stood on the tarmac, watching the helicopter rise toward the sky. It stuttered, lurched, then slammed into the mountain. In his sleep, he relived every second of the crash. The heat, the smell, the horror. He always came awake bathed in sweat, and screaming.

For the first three months after Amber had died, the nightmares had come every night. Eventually they'd slowed to once a week, then once a month. Finally they'd faded. Until he'd told Nicki the truth.

There were no words to describe the ache inside. He was empty. He hadn't thought he could hurt more than he had when he'd lost his wife and his unborn child, but he did. Because this time in addition to reliving what had been ripped from him, he'd also lost Nicki.

She was his best friend. She was his refuge. The place he could be himself. With her, there was laughter and affection and escape. They'd become friends so easily that he hadn't noticed how important she was to him until she was gone. Now he was alone and he didn't think he could face another night with the ghosts.

He grabbed his keys and walked out of his houseboat. There was only one place he knew to go.

She answered the door without asking who was there. As if she'd known it was him. As he stood on her doorstep, he took in her long red hair, the vivid green of her eyes, the perfect blush on her cheeks. He ignored the wary expression and instead saw only what they had been together. He trusted her. He didn't want to lose her. He *couldn't* lose her. But how to convince her?

"Marry me," he said without thinking. "Marry me, please. I'll do anything you want. Say anything."

She wheeled back to let him enter, then followed him to the living room.

Her steady gaze locked with his. "I'm not looking for a trained pet," she told him quietly. "If I needed someone in my life to do my bidding without question, I'd get a dog."

Her anger surprised him. Then he remembered how he'd hurt her. "I'm sorry," he told her. "I didn't mean it like that."

"Actually, I think you did." She drew in a breath. "I have a question. When the baby is born, will you care about it?"

He frowned. "Of course. It's my child."

"Will you love it?"

"Yes."

"What if we have twins?"

He stiffened. "You can't—"

She shook her head. "As far as I know, there's only one baby. Don't panic. I'm just curious. Could you love two children?"

He had no idea where she was going with this. "Sure. Why wouldn't I?"

"Because you can't love another woman. You still love Amber. So why don't you still love your unborn child?"

"That's different."

"How?"

"Isn't it obvious?"

"No," she told him. "Is it because the baby wasn't real, just like our child isn't real yet? Are you saying that you could love another child because that child hadn't been born? What if it had been? Would you open your heart to another child, having lost one?''

He shifted uncomfortably. ''What's your point?'' he asked, not sure what she was getting at, but more than a little wary about the direction they were taking. ''I want to be a father. I want to take care of both of you.''

''I appreciate that,'' she said. ''You care about me.''

He relaxed a little. ''You know I do.''

''And as a friend, you can love me, just not romantically.''

The tension returned. He sensed pitfalls but couldn't see them. ''You're very important to me.''

''Nice dodge,'' she told him. ''I'm trying to define your limits. Who can you love and under what circumstances? Because I'm not sure I believe you. That you could love more than one child. You can't love more than one woman and I don't think it's different at all. You never saw your baby with Amber, so it wasn't real to you.''

He glared at her. ''You don't understand. You weren't there.''

''I know. And watching your wife die like that had to be the most emotionally devastating event imaginable.''

He tried not to picture the explosion. ''It was worse,'' he said grimly. ''I'm the one who killed her.''

''That's where I take issue with you,'' Nicki told him. ''Unless you put a bomb on the helicopter, you *didn't* kill her any more than I did. You wanted her to leave, which made sense. There was a problem with the helicopter. It was horrible and tragic, but it wasn't your fault."

He turned away from her. "You don't know what the hell you're talking about."

"As a matter of fact, I do. It's like my skiing accident. It was awful. It changed me forever. I've been to hell and back, too, Zane. You're not the only one. The difference is I lived through it, while you're still dying every day."

"You didn't lose someone."

"I lost who I was. I lost who I could have been. I'm not saying that I don't love my life. I'm grateful I survived and that I fought back, but there was still a huge loss. I faced the demons and the fear. Sometimes they still catch me off guard. I've learned that in the past couple of days. I'll beat them down again. But what about you? Will you ever face your past? Will you ever move beyond? Because if you don't, there's no point in us continuing at all. I'm not interested in a man who lives his life ruled by fear."

Zane glared at her and swore. She didn't know. She had no right to judge him. "There isn't any fear."

"I think that's all there is. Fear that if you love again, you'll lose. It's so much easier not to try. You hide behind women who can't matter because you're terrified you'll find one who does, and then what? You'll have to risk it."

"With you?" he asked with contempt.

"With anyone." She sighed. "Ironically, knowing this about you doesn't change how I feel. I still love you. I want to be your partner, your wife and the mother of your children. But I won't be your atonement. Either you risk it all, or you get nothing. You have to be willing to take a chance."

He didn't know what to say. He couldn't think, couldn't feel. His only instinct was to run.

"I want to say I think you'll come to your senses," she said. "Unfortunately, I don't."

"I have to go," he said, rising to his feet. He headed for the door.

Before he got there, she spoke. "I'm leaving Seattle."

Zane turned and stared at her. "What?"

"I'm moving to Tucson. I can't have a real life until I get over you, and I can't see you every day at work and get over you. I'm sorry. I don't know what else to do."

Leaving? But then she would be out of his life. "When?" he asked.

"I gave my notice to Jeff this afternoon. I'm listing the house this weekend and moving in six weeks."

He reached for the doorknob. It took three tries before he was able to grasp it and escape.

He climbed into his car and headed away, driving as fast as the narrow streets would let him. Leaving. She was leaving. He tried to tell himself it was better this way. That they would get on with their lives. But he didn't believe it.

What about the baby? If she was out of state, he would never see his child, or have contact with it. Was that for the best?

He drove and drove, until he ended up by the water. Always the water. He stood at the same dock, looking out at the boats and the water. Cold seeped into his bones.

He knew what Nicki wanted, what she'd always wanted. To be someone's first choice. To be loved and cherished. But he couldn't love her. It was wrong. He still loved Amber. Amber who was...

Dead. Amber was dead.

The truth slammed into him like a runaway train. It plowed through him and over him, leaving him bent, broken and in pieces. She was dead, she was gone and she was never ever coming back. Just like their child. Just like their hopes and dreams. It was all over. It had been over for years.

But he hadn't wanted to let go, because loving her had been the best part of him. Even feeling guilty had helped keep her alive. Without her, who was he?

Staggered by the truth, he clung to the handrail. The smell of the water reminded him of a day trip he and Nicki had made to Friday Harbor. He remembered the wind tangling her hair and how she'd laughed as she rolled back and forth as the boat had rocked. That had been a good day. There had been a thousand just like them, because any day with Nicki was a good day.

At that moment Zane realized he'd been blessed twice in his life. He'd managed to find two of the most amazing women ever born and somehow they'd fallen in love with him. He'd lost one, through circumstances that weren't his fault. Was he about to lose the other because he was a horse's ass?

She deserved so much more than he could offer, but for some reason, she wanted him. How the hell had he gotten so damn lucky?

He shook his head. He'd come so close to losing her. Now all he had to do was get his sorry hide back to her place and convince her to give him another chance.

He headed for his car but before he got there,

his cell phone rang. The caller ID said the call was from Jeff.

"What's up?" he asked by way of greeting.

"Sabotini's youngest son was just kidnapped," Jeff told him. "Tim already has our gear and will meet us at the jet. Be there in twenty minutes."

Zane arrived at the airport to find the team already in place. Nicki was there with a checklist. When he walked toward her, she acknowledged him with a tight nod, then pointed to his pile of gear.

"I need you to go through that. Call out what you have and I'll note it."

He wanted to talk about something more important than whether or not he had a stun gun in his bag, but knew this wasn't the time. Whatever his personal feelings might be, or what he might have learned, Sabotini's kid was in danger and that had to be his first priority.

In less than twenty minutes, they were on the jet and taxiing down the runway.

Zane and Jeff sat together. Jeff brought him up to date on how the kidnapping had occurred. Within an hour, they were receiving information from Nicki, who had set up a command center back at the office. She fed reports frcm local law enforcement, as well as messages from resources Jeff and Zane had in Europe.

Two hours out of New York, Zane briefed the team. They had a good idea of where the boy was being held and would be going in to get him.

"What about local law enforcement?" Nicki asked, her voice only slightly scratchy after being bounced off a satellite.

"Mr. Sabotini wants us to move quickly," Jeff said. "We take orders from him."

"Don't get arrested."

"That's a secondary concern."

"I know. It's just all that bail money really cuts into petty cash."

Jeff smiled. "I'll be in touch," he said and disconnected the call. Then he turned to Zane. "Want to talk about what's up?"

Zane shrugged. Normally he was the one coordinating communications with Nicki, but this time, he'd handed the headset to Jeff.

Jeff glanced back at their team, then lowered his voice. "I know she's pregnant. She told me."

Zane wasn't surprised. "We're dealing with it."

"Not very well. She resigned."

Zane's gut tightened. She'd told him she'd done it, but he'd been hoping she'd exaggerated the truth. He should have known that wasn't her way.

"She wants to go to Tucson and live near her folks," he said.

Jeff stared at him. "What do you want?"

Nicki, Zane thought. "The situation is complicated."

"When I was being an idiot about Ashley, you told me that chances like that don't come along very often. That I had the opportunity to find normal and that I should take it."

"I remember," Zane said.

"I'm going to give that same advice back to you. You loved and lost once. Do you want to love and lose again because this time you're not willing to take a chance? To find someone you can love heart and soul is a miracle."

Zane nodded. "I've figured that much out myself. The thing is…" He couldn't believe he was about to admit this. "I'm not worth it. I don't know why the hell she cares, but she does. How am I supposed to live up to that?"

Jeff shrugged. "You can't. None of us can. Those women who love us are amazing. They don't expect perfection. All they ask for in return for their love and devotion is for us to love them back. It seems to me we're getting the better bargain, but they don't mind."

It made no sense to Zane. Yet when he thought about his conversations with Nicki, all she'd ever asked was for him to love her back. It didn't seem like nearly enough, but maybe he was making this too hard.

Before he could decide, the satellite phone rang. Zane reached for it.

"What have you got?" he asked.

Nicki blinked in surprise. She'd expected to hear Jeff's voice and she really hated that hearing Zane's made her heart thunder like a herd of buffalo.

"Infrared photos from the complex," she said. "I'm faxing them. I think we've found the boy and his kidnappers."

She heard Zane repeating the information, then the shuffling of paper.

"Got 'em," he said. "What's the word from local law enforcement?"

"They're unhappy that you've been called in. But Mr. Sabotini has some very influential friends. A call came from D.C. that you were to be given whatever backup you needed. I guess you won't be going to jail."

"Good thing. The food is lousy."

She heard muffled voices, then Zane spoke again.

"We're about twenty minutes from landing. I'll call back when we're on our way there."

"I'll be waiting." She hesitated. "Be careful."

"Always."

There was a click, then he was gone.

Nicki spent the next couple of hours relaying information to the team. She tapped into multiple computer systems and satellite systems, coordinating everything through her console. Most of the support staff had been called in.

By the time the team pulled up to within a quarter mile of the old abandoned grocery store, it was dawn on the east coast.

"The best time to attack," she murmured to herself. "It's when the enemy gets weakest."

She'd heard Zane and Jeff talk about that dozens of times and knew it to be true. Everything would be fine. Within an hour or so, the kid would be rescued and everyone would be heading home. Including Zane.

Nicki ached to see him—a real mistake considering how things were between them. She was supposed to be leaving town in an effort to get over him. Missing him after less than twelve hours didn't bode well for her recovery.

Nicki turned her attention back to the team and what was happening. They were all wearing headsets now, and she could listen to their conversations. She sent the latest infrared photos to Jeff's handheld console and talked with Zane about the temporary security system setup.

"I've tapped into it and turned it off," she said.

"The fools actually hooked it up to the phone lines, if you can believe it."

"Good work," he said. "All right everybody. Lock and load. Remember, stun weapons only. There's a kid in there. Nobody gets dead on this one."

Nicki swallowed. The decision had been made to not use bullets for fear of starting a gunfight that would take out the hostage. But that didn't mean the kidnappers would play by their rules.

Several voices came at once, then quieted as the team approached the buildings. She heard sounds of movement, the squeak of a door. Quiet voices murmured their positions.

When the action started, it was fast, confusing and left her shaking. Just like always. But this time Nicki listened for someone to say the boy was okay. She had a direct line to Mr. Sabotini, and would get to him with real-time information, just as soon as she had it.

"Got him," Zane said gruffly. "Jeez, he's maybe seven. Hey, it's all right."

She heard a child crying, then a babble of words she couldn't understand.

"Great," Zane muttered. "He doesn't speak English."

"I'm getting a patch," Nicki yelled, as she typed furiously. "Mr. Sabotini, Zane has your son, but he's terrified. He doesn't speak English. Tell him we're the good guys."

Nicki listened as father and son communicated. The relief in the older man's voice made her smile. She touched her stomach, knowing one day she would have a baby to hold and love. Pray God she was never put in Mr. Sabotini's position.

"Better," Zane said a couple of minutes later. "Jeff, we're ready. Is that all five of them?"

Nicki froze. "Zane, there's six. Remember? That one guy who's—"

Her words were cut off in a hail of gunfire. At the sound of the bullets, Nicki's heart froze. She knew, she just *knew* even before she heard Jeff yell.

"I've got the boy. Somebody grab Zane." Jeff swore. "He's been hit. Damn it all to hell."

There was more gunfire. The console blurred and Nicki realized she was crying. "No," she whispered. "Zane, no!"

"Nicki?"

She recognized his voice. Relief flooded her. "Zane? Are you okay?"

Ted's voice came over her headpiece. "He's, ah, fine, Nicki."

She knew a lie when she heard one. "Ted, you have to save him. You have to!"

"Nicki," Zane said, sounding more than a little shaky. "I'm really sorry. About everything. I know the timing really sucks on this, but I want you to know I love you. For real. For always."

She couldn't believe it. Her tears fell faster. She brushed them away and grabbed the mouthpiece. "You better mean that, Zane. And you'd better come back here alive or I'll never forgive you."

She felt someone crouch next to her and turned to find Brenda. The older woman pulled her close.

"I'm sure he'll be fine," she said.

Nicki nodded because she couldn't speak. The sound of a helicopter filled her headset, then she heard nothing at all.

*   *   *

Six hours later, Nicki was back on the airport tarmac. Jeff had called to say Zane was going to be okay and that they were heading home. The kidnappers had been arrested and were already giving the names of their leaders. The law enforcement officials figured it would only take a couple of days to round everyone up.

A grateful Mr. Sabotini had promised to visit Seattle to thank the team in person…but not for a few days. Right now he wanted to be with his family.

Nicki could relate to that. She only wanted to see Zane. Apparently he'd insisted on flying home rather than checking into a hospital, so she knew he was conscious, but she didn't know how bad his injury was. Zane could be five kinds of stubborn.

Just in case, she had a private ambulance standing by and had already plotted the quickest route to the nearest hospital. As for herself, she was numb. His last words, that he loved her, echoed in her mind. If they were true—please God, let them be true—then she had everything she'd ever wanted in life.

It seemed like hours before the plane finally appeared in the sky, then landed and taxied to where she was sitting. The doors opened. Jeff came out first. She searched his face, hoping for some clue to Zane's condition, but her boss's features were annoyingly blank. She braced herself for a stretcher, for blood, for something really horrible, then nearly passed out when Zane appeared at the top of the stairs.

He actually walked down himself. Unaided. Her gaze narrowed as she took in the sling he wore and the flew specks of blood on his shirt.

"That's it?" she screeched. "You're barely shot at all?"

He grinned sheepishly as he approached. "I sort of got winged during the gunfight. At first it looked a lot worse than it was."

She was both furious and relieved. "You made me suffer," she told him. "Dammit, Zane, I thought you were going to die."

He walked over and crouched in front of her.

"Never," he said, taking her hands in his. "I don't want to leave you." He stared into her eyes. "I might have exaggerated my condition to get the sympathy vote, but everything else I said was a hundred percent true. I love you, Nicki."

She gazed at him. "What about Amber? What about the past?"

"I loved her, and some part of me will always care about her. But she's my past and you're my future. I want to love you every day of my life. I want us to have children together, to be happy, to grow old. I love you, Nicki, more than I can ever tell you."

The last of her doubts and fears faded away. She leaned toward him. "Then I guess you're going to have to show me."

He smiled. "Gladly. As often as you'd like." He kissed her. "I still want to marry you, but for different reasons. I'll understand if you want a little time so I can prove myself."

"I might make you wait a day or two until I say yes."

They kissed again, slowly, deeply, ignoring the movement around them as the jet was unloaded. Finally Zane raised his head.

"Let's get out of here," he said. "Back to your place where we can have a serious reunion."

"Do we need to stop by the hospital so you can get some stitches?"

"I'm fine. More than fine." He touched her cheek. "I'll go anywhere you want, Nicki. If moving to Tucson is important to you, I'll go."

She shook her head. "I'd rather stay here," she told him. "It's where we belong."

He stood and walked beside her as she moved to her van. "So who do you like for the game on Sunday?" he asked

She started laughing. "You never learn, do you?"

He smiled. "You're wrong. I've learned the most important lesson of all. But I still believe I can beat you in a football pool."

"In your dreams, big guy. In your dreams."

Epilogue

Christmas—2028

Christmas Greetings from the Rankin family. Once again, we're thrilled to bring our loved ones up to date on the happenings in the household.

Starting with the youngest member of the family—Zoe is a senior in high school. She's—if you'll excuse the pun—kicking butt on her soccer team and it looks like she's going to be offered several athletic scholarships at various colleges. She still hates math, loves history and has had seven boyfriends this year. It is a record, even for her. Zane says it's because she's as pretty as her mother. Zoe says it's because she's also very picky.

Sean is in his last year at the University of Washington where he will graduate with a degree in chemical engineering. He still plans to go on to get his Ph.D., which his sisters find really scary. Sean has a ''serious'' girlfriend, but says we're not allowed to talk about her in the newsletter.

When he's not studying, Sean spends his time boating and plans to crew on an entry in the next America's Cup.

April and her new husband are blissfully happy. After six months of marriage, they swear they'd do it all over again, which is lovely to hear. April is still enjoying the law and plans to make partner before she turns thirty. Charlie, her husband, has two more years of his pediatric residency left before he can hang out his shingle.

As for Nicki and Zane, we celebrated our twenty-fifth wedding anniversary with a month-long trip to Australia. The security firm is still successful and growing, although rumors that the president insisted on members of the Ritter/Rankin team accompanying her on her Far East tour are slightly exaggerated.

Nicki's computer firm has doubled in size…again.

The entire family feels blessed by the love they share. We all send holiday greetings to you and yours. May all your dreams come true.

* * * * *

Don't miss Susan Mallery's
next compelling story,
EXPECTING!
The first title in
Silhouette Special Edition's new
MERLYN COUNTY MIDWIVES *continuity.*
Available in January 2004.

A LITTLE BIT PREGNANT—
Readers' Ring
Discussion Questions:

1. Nicki being in a wheelchair is an important element of this story. Would the book have worked as well without that element?

2. In many romances the characters are physically perfect. Is that an important part of the fantasy/reading experience for you? Why?

3. How do you feel about characters with disabilities? Do they make you uncomfortable?

4. *A Little Bit Pregnant* takes place in Seattle. Do you think of that as a fun, romantic city? What cities are the most romantic?

5. Nicki and Zane make love on the sofa. Other than the bedroom, what rooms are the most fun for making love? What room would really turn you off?

6. Zane is keeping a secret from his past. What is the worst secret a boyfriend or husband has ever kept from you? Are you keeping any secrets?

7. In *A Little Bit Pregnant*, Zane feels guilt about his late wife's death. Has grief ever played a role in your romantic life?

8. When is it all right for a character to let go of the past and move on? Do you have different expectations for characters than you do for "real" people?

9. Nicki and Zane are good friends who become lovers. Have you ever had the experience of falling in love with a friend?

10. Every major character in a romance has an emotional "flaw." How do these "flaws" make people right for each other?

11. This book has a unique epilogue. Did you enjoy finding out about the characters' future in that way? Do you like epilogues that wrap up all the loose ends and "prove" the happily-ever-after ending?

12. In the beginning of the story, Nicki thinks of Zane as the one man she'll never have. Do you have a "one who got away"?

13. If you were to star in your own romance novel, who would you be? Who is your perfect hero?

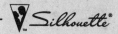

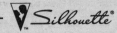

Your opinion is important to us! Please take a few moments to share your thoughts with us about your experiences with Harlequin and Silhouette books. Your comments will be very useful in ensuring that we deliver books you love to read.
Please take a few minutes to complete the questionnaire, then send it to us at the address below.

Send your completed questionnaires to:
Harlequin/Silhouette Reader Survey, P.O. Box 9046, Buffalo, NY 14269-9046

---

1. As you may know, there are many different lines under the Harlequin and Silhouette brands. Each of the lines is listed below. Please check the box that most represents your reading habit for each line.

Line	Currently read this line	Do not read this line	Not sure if I read this line
Harlequin American Romance	❑	❑	❑
Harlequin Duets	❑	❑	❑
Harlequin Romance	❑	❑	❑
Harlequin Historicals	❑	❑	❑
Harlequin Superromance	❑	❑	❑
Harlequin Intrigue	❑	❑	❑
Harlequin Presents	❑	❑	❑
Harlequin Temptation	❑	❑	❑
Harlequin Blaze	❑	❑	❑
Silhouette Special Edition	❑	❑	❑
Silhouette Romance	❑	❑	❑
Silhouette Intimate Moments	❑	❑	❑
Silhouette Desire	❑	❑	❑

2. Which of the following best describes why you bought *this book?* One answer only, please.

the picture on the cover	❑	the title	❑
the author	❑	the line is one I read often	❑
part of a miniseries	❑	saw an ad in another book	❑
saw an ad in a magazine/newsletter	❑	a friend told me about it	❑
I borrowed/was given this book	❑	other: _____	❑

3. Where did you buy *this book?* One answer only, please.

at Barnes & Noble	❑	at a grocery store	❑
at Waldenbooks	❑	at a drugstore	❑
at Borders	❑	on eHarlequin.com Web site	❑
at another bookstore	❑	from another Web site	❑
at Wal-Mart	❑	Harlequin/Silhouette Reader	❑
at Target	❑	Service/through the mail	
at Kmart	❑	used books from anywhere	❑
at another department store or mass merchandiser	❑	I borrowed/was given this book	❑

4. On average, how many Harlequin and Silhouette books do you buy at one time?

I buy _____ books at one time	❑
I rarely buy a book	❑

MRQ403SSE-1A

5. How many times per month do you shop for any *Harlequin and/or Silhouette* books?
   One answer only, please.

1 or more times a week	❏	a few times per year	❏
1 to 3 times per month	❏	less often than once a year	❏
1 to 2 times every 3 months	❏	never	❏

6. When you think of your ideal heroine, which *one* statement describes her the best?
   One answer only, please.

She's a woman who is strong-willed	❏	She's a desirable woman	❏
She's a woman who is needed by others	❏	She's a powerful woman	❏
She's a woman who is taken care of	❏	She's a passionate woman	❏
She's an adventurous woman		She's a sensitive woman	❏

7. The following statements describe types or genres of books that you may be
   interested in reading. Pick *up to 2 types* of books that you are most interested in.

I like to read about truly romantic relationships	❏
I like to read stories that are sexy romances	❏
I like to read romantic comedies	❏
I like to read a romantic mystery/suspense	❏
I like to read about romantic adventures	❏
I like to read romance stories that involve family	❏
I like to read about a romance in times or places that I have never seen	❏
Other: _____	❏

*The following questions help us to group your answers with those readers who are
similar to you. Your answers will remain confidential.*

8. Please record your year of birth below.
   19 ____

9. What is your marital status?
   single ❏   married ❏   common-law ❏   widowed ❏
   divorced/separated ❏

10. Do you have children 18 years of age or younger currently living at home?
    yes ❏   no ❏

11. Which of the following best describes your employment status?
    employed full-time or part-time ❏   homemaker ❏   student ❏
    retired ❏   unemployed ❏

12. Do you have access to the Internet from either home or work?
    yes ❏   no ❏

13. Have you ever visited eHarlequin.com?
    yes ❏   no ❏

14. What state do you live in?
    _____

15. Are you a member of Harlequin/Silhouette Reader Service?
    yes ❏   Account # _____   no ❏   MRQ403SSE-1B